THE MEDUSA PROJECT
HIT SQUAD

Award-winning books from Sophie McKenzie

GIRL, MISSING

Winner Richard and Judy Best Kids' Books 2007 12+
Winner of the Red House Children's Book Award 2007 12+
Winner of the Manchester Children's Book Award 2008
Winner of the Bolton Children's Book Award 2007
Winner of the Grampian Children's Book Award 2008
Winner of the John Lewis Solihull Book Award 2008
Winner of the Lewisham Children's Book Award 2009
Winner of the 2008 Sakura Medal

SIX STEPS TO A GIRL

Winner of the Manchester Children's Book Award 200█

BLOOD TIES

Overall winner of the Red House Children's Book Award 2█
Winner of the North East Teenage Book Award 2010
Winner of the Leeds Book Award 2009 age 11-14 categor█
Winner of the Spellbinding Award 2009
Winner of the Lancashire Children's Book Award 2009
Winner of the Portsmouth Book Award 2009 (Longer Novel section)
Winner of the Staffordshire Children's Book Award 2009
Winner of the Southern Schools Book Award 2010
Winner of the RED Book Award 2010
Winner of the Warwickshire Secondary Book Award 2010
Winner of the Grampian Children's Book Award 2010
Winner of the North East Teenage Book Award 2010

THE MEDUSA PROJECT: THE SET-UP

Winner of the North-East Book Award 2010
Winner of the Portsmouth Book Award 2010
Winner of the Yorkshire Coast Book Award 2010

SOPHIE McKENZIE

THE MEDUSA PROJECT
HIT SQUAD

SIMON AND SCHUSTER

First published in Great Britain in 2012 by Simon and Schuster UK Ltd
A CBS COMPANY

Copyright © 2012 Sophie McKenzie

Simon & Schuster UK Ltd
1st Floor, 222 Gray's Inn Road, London WC1X 8HB

A CIP catalogue record for this book
is available from the British Library.

PB ISBN: 978-0-85707-071-5
E-BOOK ISBN: 978-0-85707-072-2

1 3 5 7 9 10 8 6 4 2

Printed and bound by CPI Group (UK) Ltd, Croydon, CR0 4YY

www.simonandschuster.co.uk
www.sophiemckenziebooks.com

For Lou Kuenzler

Fourteen years ago, scientist William Fox implanted four babies with the Medusa gene – a gene for psychic abilities. Fox's experiment left a legacy: four teenagers – Nico, Ketty, Ed and Fox's own daughter, Dylan – who have each developed their own distinct and special skill.

Initially, the four worked together as the Medusa Project – a secret, government-funded, crime-fighting force. However, after learning that their mentor had betrayed them, the Medusa teens fled the country. On the run, they discovered the existence of two other young people with the Medusa gene: Cal – Nico's half-brother – who can fly, and Amy – Ed's sister – a shapeshifter.

Temporarily based in Australia, various factions are now battling for control of the teenagers' lives. Their parents, who want to separate them and hide them away with new lives and identities, face opposition from the government, which is keen to make fresh use of their psychic skills.

However, Nico, Ketty, Ed and Dylan are determined to investigate claims that a drug conveying the same abilities as the Medusa gene has been developed – and are making plans of their own ...

KETTY

1: The Getaway

The night sky over the ranch was full of stars, but I wasn't looking up. I was leading the way to our meeting place with the others. I stopped at the end of the porch and took a couple of steadying breaths. I was desperate to see into the next few minutes. That's my particular Medusa ability... visions of the future.

But, as so often when I'm feeling stressed, I couldn't see anything.

'What is it, Ketty?' Ed whispered behind me.

I shook my head, glad that he wasn't attempting to read my mind. 'Nothing.'

I hoped it didn't matter that I couldn't see if there were any obstacles to our escape. We were on the trail of a drug – Medusix – that mimicked our genetically-given psychic skills and it was important we got away from here tonight. In the morning our parents, in an effort to prevent the UK government from taking charge of us again, were planning to separate us from each other and send us on different flights all over the world.

'Er ... come on, Ketty, the others will be waiting,' Ed whispered. He ran his hand anxiously through his sandy, tufty hair. 'Ketty?'

I peered round the corner of the porch. It was nearly 3 a.m. and the ranch house was dark and silent. The night air was still and cool. Apart from the moon and stars above, the only light came from the lanterns that illuminated the exit – across the field to our right. We were heading in the opposite direction.

'Okay, let's go.' With a final glance back at the ranch I raced across the field on our left, Ed by my side. We were due to meet the others at 3 a.m. in the paddock. As we neared the paddock fence I could just make out Dylan's profile. She was leaning against the gate stroking one of the horses in the field. Nico stood beside her. He caught sight of me and beckoned us over. I could see the tension on his face as we ran up. He turned to Ed.

'Where's your sister?' he demanded. 'Where's Amy?'

'Er ...' Ed stammered.

'We didn't bring her,' I said quickly. Confessing that Amy wasn't with us was what I'd been nervous about, much more than running away from the ranch. Ed and I had decided to leave her behind ... that she'd be safer staying with the adults.

'*What?*' Nico's mouth fell open. 'But we agreed.'

'No we didn't.' I stood my ground. '*You* were the only

4

person who wanted Amy along. You ordered Ed to tell her where to meet but Ed never actually said he would do it.'

When the four of us had discussed ways of leaving the house, neither Cal nor Amy had been present. Nico had talked to Cal later about his role in our escape but he'd told Ed to tell Amy about our plans.

Neither Ed nor I had spoken up against this at the time, though it was obvious from the look on Ed's face that he disliked Nico's order as much as I did.

'Amy's too young,' Ed protested, finding his voice at last. 'She's three years younger than we are.'

Nico turned his gaze to me. 'Ketts? What's going on?'

I looked away. Things had been awkward between Nico and me for a couple of weeks now and Amy – or rather her ability to change her appearance at will – was at the heart of the problem. Basically, a few weeks ago, she'd been forced to look like me to manipulate Nico. After the danger we'd been facing had passed, Amy hadn't changed back to herself straight away. She'd waited a few minutes ... letting Nico kiss her while he still thought she was me. I didn't really blame Amy for that. She was young and my boyfriend is gorgeous – all dark eyes, silky hair and charming smile.

No, I blamed Nico for encouraging her to have a huge crush on him. He'd flirted with her like mad for ages. Not because he particularly liked her – but just because he could. It was typical Nico behaviour ... egotistical and thoughtless ... and I was fed up with it.

'Excuse me,' drawled Dylan. She moved away from the

5

horse she was stroking and stood between us. The moonlight picked out the tiny white-gold stud in her nose. She'd only had the piercing done last week and it kind of suited her hard-faced prettiness. 'This is no time for a tiff. If you wanna know what *I* think, we're totally better off without Princess Ten-Faces, but the important thing is that we get out of here.' She peered towards the ranch. 'Where *is* Cal anyway? He should be here by now.'

Nico's jaw tightened. 'I'm going back for Amy,' he said. 'It's not fair to leave her out – and we need her Medusa skill. It's just as valuable as any of ours.' He paused. 'And more reliable than some.'

I winced. This was, I was sure, a dig at my own flaky ability to see into the future. Beside me, Ed's face reddened. He hates it when we all argue.

Dylan grabbed Nico's arm. 'You can't go back. Cal will be here any second. And if we're caught trying to leave they'll watch over us till morning and then we'll *never* get away.'

'Remember what we need to do,' I insisted. 'We have to find out if Medusix really exists . . . if anyone's used it yet. It's going to be a really dangerous mission.'

'Ketty's right,' Ed added. 'It's too risky for Amy.'

I could see Nico wavering. Like the rest of us he had been shocked at our recent discovery that Geri Paterson – the government agent who brought us together as the Medusa Project – was a murderer who had tried to kill us. Two weeks ago, in a terrible showdown at the ranch, Geri had herself been killed in front of us. The images were still seared onto my mind and I knew they'd affected Nico deeply as well. The situation we were heading into could easily be just as dangerous.

'I still think Amy could be useful,' Nico said stubbornly.

Something snapped inside me. 'Useful as a boost to your massive ego, you mean?' I said.

'Oooh, someone's jealous.' Dylan suppressed a giggle.

An awkward silence fell. I looked away.

'Look!' At the sound of Ed's voice I spun round. He was pointing towards the ranch house. A light had been switched on inside and a slight figure in jeans was racing towards us across the field. It was Cal, Nico's half-brother.

'At last,' Dylan muttered.

As Cal drew closer, another light came on in the house.

'Man, those lights are coming from our bedrooms.' Nico turned on me and Ed, furious. 'How much noise did you make leaving?'

'None,' Ed protested.

'Stop picking on us, Nico,' I said.

He glared at me as Cal raced up. He was slightly out of breath from running, his white-blond hair and pale face contrasting dramatically with his dark clothes.

'Come on,' he gasped, his Australian accent strong in his voice. 'We have to hurry. They know we're gone. They'll be out here any sec.'

'We still need to fetch Amy,' Nico said. 'I can get in and out fast and—'

'No way,' Cal interrupted. 'It was Amy who sounded the alarm. She woke up and saw everyone was gone. She assumed someone had kidnapped us.'

Nico swore. Dylan's eyes widened.

'Didn't you think to leave a note for your sister, Chino Boy?' she asked Ed.

'I *did*,' Ed blustered. 'She obviously hasn't seen it yet in the dark and—'

'Will you all shut up,' Cal hissed. 'We need to go. Right now.' He extended his arms. I took hold of one hand, Dylan the other.

Nico took a step back. 'I'm telling you this is a mistake,' he said.

'Come on, Nico, please.' I held out my other hand to him.

For a second, Nico looked at me. His eyes, even in the darkness, were full of emotion: part frustration, part anger ... part disappointment. He didn't speak but I could read his thoughts as powerfully as if I were Ed.

You've let me down, Ketty.

I was still holding out my hand, waiting for him to take it. When Cal was using his Medusa gift with the four of us, we always travelled in the same formation: me and Nico on one side; Dylan and Ed on the other.

Shouts were now audible from the house. There was Fergus, Dylan's uncle, shouting all our names ... and Amy, calling for Ed ... and Nico.

'Come on, mate,' Cal urged.

With a growl, Nico gave in. My hand was still outstretched,

but he pointedly walked away from me, to Cal's other side, and took Dylan's hand.

It felt like a punch in the guts.

The atmosphere tensed further.

'Ed, mate, get in line,' Cal snapped.

Ed, who'd been watching the scene between Nico and me with gaping mouth, stepped over and took my hand. As the five of us stood in a row, ready to take off, Ed squeezed my fingers. I gave his hand a squeeze back to acknowledge his kindness, but inside it made no difference. Inside I was devastated.

'Ready?' Cal glanced up and down the line.

We all nodded. No one spoke. The yells from the ranch house were louder now. Out of the corner of my eye, I could just make out Fergus racing across the field in our direction.

'No!' he yelled. 'Stop!'

With a sudden jerk, Cal yanked on my hand. My feet left the ground and a moment later we soared into the night sky.

2: The Arrival

We didn't speak as we flew. Cal and Ed, on either side of me, weren't ignoring me or being unkind, but Ed hates being up in the air, so he spent the entire journey with his eyes tight shut, and Cal kept quiet because he has to concentrate when he's flying. He has an amazing ability – personally I think it's the coolest Medusa skill, not that I'd ever say so to the others. I mean, mine is frustrating and unpredictable and I know Ed often hates being able to read minds. But Dylan and Nico love what they can do.

As we soared over the rough, rugged Australian landscape, I realised that Cal's ability to fly was special because he could extend it to others. This was true of Dylan's protective force, of course. She'd recently learned how to protect others as well as herself. And Cal helped other people have fun. In contrast, Nico's telekinesis was kind of a selfish ability. Sure he could move objects to fight off external threats, and he'd saved all our lives on more than one occasion, but that was in rare and extreme situations. Most of the time he only used his telekinesis to show off.

For the first time it struck me that maybe the showing off was part of a deeper problem ... that maybe Nico was just fundamentally very selfish. Not merely a bit self-centred, like most people probably are, but truly egotistical through and through.

I looked down at the desert landscape over which we were flying. The sun was rising now and the sky was a blazing fire of red and orange. We were high up and I could see for miles. A small town nestled at the base of a hill to the east. A range of mountains ran along the horizon to the west. Normally this would have thrilled me. I'd always loved being up in the skies before, the wind rushing through my hair.

But today I felt empty and sad. I wanted to be on this mission, for sure, not packed off to Singapore to live with Mum and Dad and my brother Lex. But I hated how things were with Nico.

I felt a tug on my hand and looked round. Cal was indicating the ground. We'd been flying for several hours and I knew he would be getting tired. I nodded, and he shifted the angle of his body so that we began our descent. A couple of minutes later we landed in a deserted field. It was greener than most of the landscape we'd flown over and the grass felt damp around my ankles. Ed came to ground with a groan. He staggered a few paces, then slumped onto the wet grass, his head in his hands.

Letting go of Cal's hand, I walked over. 'You okay, Ed?'

He nodded, but his face was at the grey end of pale.

'Why have we stopped?' Nico said behind me, an imperious tone to his voice.

Wasn't it *obvious*?

'Because Cal needs a break and Ed feels sick,' I snapped, turning round.

Nico glared at me. With the dawn sun lighting his face, he looked absolutely beautiful. And yet his dark eyes were cold.

'Right.' He sounded like he was sneering. 'Well, we can't stop for long.'

Exasperated, I walked over to Cal. He was standing to one side, his face tipped up to the sun. 'How are you doing?' I asked.

'I'm fine.' He smiled at me, a lovely warm grin. 'Thanks, Ketty.' He slicked his hands through his blond hair. Cal was pretty good-looking himself. Not, maybe, in the same league as Nico, but definitely fit. And he liked me, I was sure he did.

I looked round. Dylan was gazing at me, eyebrows raised. I wondered what she was thinking. There was no point asking, of course. Dylan was as prickly as a rose bush. And, usually, just as glamorous, though right now – with her tousled hair and dark shadows under her pale green eyes – she did not look her best.

For a second, I thought she was going to say something about me and Cal or me and Nico, but instead she made a face and held out her long red ponytail.

'I love flying but it's *real* bad for my hair,' she drawled.

Cal and I laughed.

'Let's eat and drink something,' Cal suggested. 'I'll be ready to go again in about ten minutes.'

Dylan took off her backpack and started handing out the bottles of juice we'd packed the night before. Ed was on his feet now, looking less pale. Nico had wandered across our field to a line of trees. Once upon a time I'd have followed him, eager to put right whatever was wrong between us, but right now I felt too annoyed.

I took a bottle of orange juice and strolled in the opposite direction from Nico. Now we were under way, I felt strangely relaxed. I knew it wouldn't last. Our plan was to head for the northern coast of Australia, then land-hop across the islands of Indonesia until we reached the Asian mainland. It sounded like a holiday, but we were on a mission and there was no time to stop. Once we got as far as India, Cal was aiming to get us to Kima, in northern Europe, in a series of flying stints. Cal anticipated that the whole journey would take us a couple of days.

Kima was the source of our one and only lead. From computer files we'd found, we knew that Medusix was being developed there, and Ed and I had been checking the internet every day for reports of anything suspicious happening in the region. Two days ago we'd stumbled across a small online report from a local news station, about some bizarre-sounding occurrences in Lovistov, a small town in the south of Kima. In one instance a passengerless car with the engine off had apparently moved – almost glided, the witness statement

13

said – across a supermarket car park. In another, a set of workman's tools had appeared to dance around each other in mid-air. No one was anywhere near them at the time. Again, there was nothing conclusive to go on, but both sounded like possible demonstrations of telekinesis. Proof, perhaps, that Medusix was in use here.

Whatever the truth, once we were in Lovistov, everyone would be relying on me to have a vision of the specific place we needed to go to. Up until right now, I'd really been feeling the pressure, but this place we'd landed in was so peaceful, it seemed to ease my anxieties.

The sun was growing stronger and the sky bluer as I looked out across the green fields ahead. The others were still chatting to each other over bottles of juice, apart from Nico who had wandered some way off to the edge of our field.

I steadied my gaze on the middle distance – a blur of green and blue. If I could see into the next few hours, it would be a massive help. I let my mind go blank, as I'd done so many times, then took my focus onto the image of us flying into Lovistov. I had no real idea what the town would look like, so I just concentrated on the name and the picture of the five of us in the sky. A few deep breaths – and lights flashed before my eyes.

It was coming. The familiar strong, sickly smell that preceded all my visions filled the air and I was there ... in the future.

Darkness. My hand in Cal's as we fly ... Landing with a

bump. Stumbling. The air is cold. The ground covered in frost.

While keeping a mental hold of what I was seeing, I encouraged the vision to skip ahead. This was a technique I'd learned recently. It gave me more control over what I was seeing, though not as much control as I would have liked.

A church spire looms overhead in the moonlight. Frost crackles under my feet. I am with others, though I can't see them.

As I tried to get a sense of who I was with in the vision, my mind, unbidden, skipped ahead again. A series of quick, dramatic images filled my inner vision.

The side of the church. Graves to the right.

Unbidden, my mind skipped ahead again. The images came thick and fast – almost too quickly for me to register them.

An uneven lane ... houses ... a large wooden door with green paint peeling off the panel. Nico's hand, twisting to undo the lock ...

Trying to slow the vision down, the images skipped ahead once more.

A cold, damp passageway ... another door ... creaking open ... a bare concrete room ... cold ... a pain in my leg ... can't breathe ... a bright light, blinding me ...

With a jolt, the vision left me. I stood, gasping for air in the middle of the field. It took a second to remember where I was. And why. I turned around. Nico had rejoined the others. They were packing their juice bottles away. Dylan

15

was slipping on the backpack. Cal beckoned me over with a smile.

'Did you see something?' he asked as I walked back. 'You looked a bit glassy-eyed earlier. I thought maybe you were going to try for a vision.'

I nodded. 'We should head for the church in Lovistov. The place we're going is nearby. It was hard to work out the sequence but I saw a large green door after I saw the church and after we'd walked down a lane of houses . . .'

'So you think the green door belongs to one of the houses?'

I nodded.

Cal looked at me, impressed. 'Wow, that's ace.'

Ed smiled. 'Well done, Ketty.'

Dylan snorted. 'It's all a bit vague, isn't it? What's behind the door?'

I shrugged. 'I don't know,' I said. 'Some sort of passage-way . . . a room. But I saw Nico unlocking the front door, so I know we go in there.'

'It's a start,' Cal insisted.

I glanced at Nico who had remained uncharacteristically silent throughout this exchange. Once he would have leaped to my defence, not left it to Cal.

'Did you see anything else?' Nico's voice was cold.

'Only that there was a frost,' I said. I decided not to mention the pain in my leg or the dazzling light. I couldn't explain either – and it was hopeless trying to get the others to understand the way my visions jumped around.

Nico offered me a curt nod. He said nothing.

And when, a few minutes later, we flew on again, he stood once more beside Dylan, not me.

The rest of the journey was uneventful. Once we reached the coast, Cal rested again. Then we flew on, over Indonesia and Cambodia, too high up to make out anything distinct in the landscape. We stopped to eat and sleep only in short bursts but it was nearly dawn the following day when we arrived in Lovistov. Taking into account the time difference, Cal had been flying us for over forty-eight hours and was practically dead on his feet. He landed us – more raggedly than usual – in a copse on the edge of town. The church spire I'd seen in my vision was visible in the distance and the air was as cold as my vision had suggested. Once we reached the church, I knew the house with the green door would be close by.

Nico immediately took charge. 'Okay, Cal and Ed stay here to rest. I'll go with Dylan and Ketty to scout around. See if we can locate the house Ketty saw.'

'Any more clues for us, Ketty?' Dylan drawled.

I shook my head. I'd been trying to have another vision for most of the past two hours, but I was too stressed now. Nothing was coming.

'Great,' Dylan said sarcastically.

'I'm not staying behind,' Cal said stubbornly.

Nico sighed. 'Come on, man, you're exhaust—'

'No, I'm coming with.'

For a second, Nico and Cal glared at each other. Then

17

Nico shook his head. 'All right, but we don't want too many people wandering about, drawing attention to ourselves, so Dylan, you'll have to stay here with Ed.'

'Fine with me,' Dylan yawned, settling herself against a tree.

Nico checked his watch. 'Ed, give us ten minutes, then contact me with remote telepathy. Okay?'

Ed agreed and Nico, Cal and I set off. The night air was freezing cold. Our thin jackets – which were all we'd needed in sunny Sydney – only offered limited warmth. We walked single file, the only sound the crunching of the frosted grass under our feet. In a few minutes we reached the church I'd seen in my vision. An unevenly laid road led off on the right. I was sure it was the one from my vision. The large green door had to be along here somewhere. My confidence soared.

'Down there,' I said.

We headed over. My breath was coming fast and shallow, a white mist around my head. We reached the top of the road. The whole town felt completely deserted.

'Which door is it?' Cal whispered.

I looked up and down the street. It wasn't a long road and all the doors were painted a dull brown. I'd been wrong. The door from my vision wasn't here after all.

'It's not the right street,' I whispered.

Nico rolled his eyes. I didn't say anything to his face, but inside I was feeling annoyed. Why did he have to act so superior? Didn't he understand my Medusa ability wasn't a precise or controllable gift?

18

I opened my mouth to protest that we just needed to retrace our steps and try another street, when heavy foot-steps sounded behind us.

I spun around. Two men – burly and unsmiling – were just a few metres behind us. They stopped as we stopped. One of them barked something at the other in a foreign language.

'Looks like we've chosen the wrong hood to make a mistake in,' Cal hissed.

Nico smiled at the men. He raised his hands. 'Hi,' he said.

The two men looked at each other. One, the taller of the two, gave a menacing, gap-toothed grin.

And then he drew a knife.

3: The Patrol

The man held the knife out towards us.

'Stop,' he said with a strong eastern European accent.

'Oh man, they want to rob us,' Nico groaned.

I stared at the knife, my heart beating fast. Why couldn't I have seen this in my vision earlier? Then we could have avoided it.

Cal looked at me, his eyebrows raised. He edged closer and I realised he was trying to suggest we made a run for it ... that he could fly us into the air and we could get away.

It made sense, but Nico was already ahead of us, arms outstretched. At first I thought he was trying to snatch the man's knife using telekinesis, then I realised his hands were open in a gesture of surrender – he was trying to talk to the two men. I gulped. Nico obviously felt more confident than I did right now.

Both men looked mean: the one with the knife was short and balding, with stubble over his chin; the other was taller and thinner, with a broken nose that gave his face a squashed look.

'We don't have any money with us,' Nico said. 'We're just here trying to find out about some strange things that have been happening.'

Knife Man narrowed his eyes.

'What strange things?' he said suspiciously.

My heart skipped a beat. The man was still clutching his knife. Was he holding it too tightly for Nico to teleport it away if he needed to?

'Weird stuff,' Nico said. 'There was a car that moved without a driver. Some tools that spun in the air.'

The two men stared at him blankly. Knife Man turned to Broken Nose with raised eyebrows. '*These* sound crazy things.'

Broken Nose shook his head. 'You must come with us.'

'No,' Nico insisted. He raised his hands again and, this time, I was certain he was going to try and whip Knife Man's weapon away using telekinesis.

But before Nico could act, Knife Man leaped forward. He grabbed my arm and twisted me round. I felt the cold press of metal on my skin. Cal and Nico stared, helpless, at the blade against my throat.

I froze.

'You come with us,' Knife Man said.

My stomach lurched, sickeningly, into my chest.

Nico thrust out his hand and twisted it. He was definitely trying to wrench the knife away using telekinesis, but the

21

man was gripping it too hard. Cal hesitated, clearly torn between flying away to sound the alarm and staying to help me.

'Don't hurt her,' he cried out.

'Move,' Broken Nose ordered. 'Or we kill the girl.'

Knife Man spun me around, his weapon still against my throat. He shoved me forward.

I had no choice but to let him lead us away.

I stumbled across the road, the knife cold on my skin. I didn't dare look round to see if the others were okay. Both boys were talking at once, Nico demanding that the men let us go and Cal simply imploring them not to hurt me.

A moment later we were back at the road opposite the church. The town was starting to stir, the morning air crisp and clear. A woman appeared outside a house with a basketful of washing to hang on the line. When she saw us, she scuttled back inside. As we passed the church, I glanced along the far side of the building.

The large green door from my vision was *there*.

'No.' The word burst out of me. Why hadn't I insisted we looked around here properly before? I'd been so certain that my vision had skipped ahead from the church to a different place entirely, I hadn't considered that the green door might simply be on a different part of the building.

'What's the matter?' Nico asked urgently.

'The green door I saw earlier,' I said. 'It's on the side of the church.'

'Quiet.' Knife Man pressed the metal tip of his weapon against my throat. I gasped with terror, my mind spinning. In trying to find out about Medusix we appeared to have walked into another, equally dangerous, situation.

'Where are you taking us?' Cal demanded.

'Silence,' Broken Nose ordered.

I chewed anxiously on my lip. We'd left Ed and Dylan back by the trees just a moment ago. Ed would attempt to contact us by remote telepathy in a few minutes. Unless Nico and Cal could somehow get the knife off my captor, he was our best chance for escape.

We left the church behind and turned onto a street full of shops and cafés. Most of these were either closed or boarded-up. Knife Man pushed me inside the second café on the right. It was empty – a small room with a bar and food counter at one end and a clutch of tables and chairs by the window.

Across the room and down some stairs to a cellar. In the sudden darkness I could just make out a dusty space filled with crates and boxes, then through to the tiny, empty room behind. Knife Man shoved me through the door. I spun round in time to see Nico and Cal being hurled in after me and then the door slammed shut on us with a bang.

We were locked in.

Cal rushed over. 'Ketts, are you all right?' I nodded.

Nico thumped the door with his fist. 'Let us out!' he yelled.

I looked around. The room was completely bare – stone

23

floors and concrete walls painted a dirty shade of grey. It wasn't large – maybe three metres square. And there was just one small window, high up on the far wall. Cal followed my gaze. A second later he zoomed off the ground. He hovered, two metres off the ground, peering closely at the glass. He prodded the handle with his fingers.

'Locked,' he said.

'Get me up there,' Nico ordered. 'I'll sort that.' He grinned at me. 'Lucky you're here with me rather than Ed or Dylan.'

'Or Amy,' I said.

The smile fell from Nico's face at this reminder of our earlier argument.

Cal swooped down and grabbed Nico by the arm. 'Come on,' he said.

'What d'you think's going on?' I asked. 'If those men just wanted money they'd have mugged us. Why have they brought us here?'

'It doesn't matter,' Nico said sharply as he soared up behind Cal. 'We just need to get out of here and get back to the mission. All that matters is finding out if someone's really developed Medusix.'

'I know that's the priority,' I said, just as sharply back. 'I'm just asking.'

Up in the air, Nico twisted his hand and the lock on the small window clicked free. With a creak, the window itself opened.

'It leads straight onto the pavement outside,' Nico said.

24

'Right, you go through,' Cal said. 'Then I'll go down and fetch Ketty.'

Both boys looked down at me. I nodded.

Cal carefully hovered closer to the window, moving his hold from Nico's arm to round his waist, then positioning Nico so that he could crawl through the narrow opening. Nico reached through with his head and arms. I watched, holding my breath as he gradually disappeared from view. Cal stayed beside him, guiding his lower body.

The bolts on the other side of the door rattled as someone dragged them back. Cal caught my eye. He was still pushing Nico through the window. He looked terrified. A key turned in the lock.

'Go!' I hissed at Cal. 'Come back for me in a minute.'

Cal shoved Nico fully through the window, but didn't follow himself.

'Come on, Ketts,' he hissed, one hand clinging on to the window ledge, the other reaching down for me.

The door handle started to turn. 'No, there's no time. Come back for me.' With a grimace, Cal slithered through the opening – and I faced the door.

Broken Nose stood in front of me. His mouth gaped as he took in the empty room. He looked up at the open window and shouted something in a language I didn't understand. I heard Knife Man pounding up the stairs to the ground floor.

I held my breath, hoping Cal and Nico had enough time to get away.

Broken Nose and I stared at each other. I took a step away from him. Hopefully Cal and Nico were hiding outside, around the corner. As soon as Broken Nose left me again, Cal could come back and fetch me.

But Broken Nose didn't leave me. Instead he grabbed my arm and dragged me from the room. I tried to resist. He shouted. Then he opened the door of a tiny cupboard. It contained a mop and bucket full of cleaning rags and bottles, plus a ladder. Broken Nose shoved me inside. I fell against the ladder. The door slammed shut.

I stood gasping with the shock. My arm hurt where I'd landed on the rungs of the ladder. But worse, far worse, was the fact that the cupboard was pitch black.

And that I was now completely alone.

4: The Trap

I banged on the door, panic rising and whirling inside me. It's not that I'm afraid of the dark, but the cupboard was tiny. Worse, no one knew I was here. If Cal and Nico did manage to escape Knife Man and come back, they would have no idea where to find me.

Well, I'd just have to make sure they heard me. I thumped on the door again, yelling at the top of my voice.

'Let me out! Help!'

I shouted for a whole minute, then I stopped and listened. I could hear nothing outside. I took a few deep breaths, trying to calm myself. Perhaps if I looked a little way into the future, I would see the boys coming back to rescue me.

The thought of this was reassuring. I steadied my gaze into the darkness. It really was completely black inside the cupboard. No light at all shone in from outside, which meant the doors out of the basement must all be shut. Probably locked. It didn't matter. Nico would be able to handle the locks.

Focus, I told myself sternly. *Stop rushing ahead in your mind and let it take you* properly *into the future. Just the next few minutes. Just a little way.*

I stood as still as I could, keeping my breathing steady. My heart was still racing. I tried to switch my panicking brain off . . . to let go. But it was impossible.

A sob rose up inside me.

Now I felt like a failure too.

I gulped back the tears. There was no point feeling sorry for myself. I had to find some way out of here. I cast around the cupboard, feeling the contents carefully. All I'd seen in the split second when the door had opened was the ladder and the mop and bucket. But maybe there were other items too. Maybe even something I could use to break the door's lock. I felt along the floor behind me. It was made of stone, like the passageway outside, and cold to the touch.

And then, without warning, Ed's voice appeared in my head.

Ketty, are you all right?

A huge smile broke out on my face. In my terrible state of panic, I'd forgotten that Ed had recently developed the ability to communicate remotely with the rest of us with the Medusa gene. Suddenly I knew I wasn't alone. They were all behind me. And Ed . . . my dearest friend, who is like a brother to me, was right here, right now.

Knowing Ed could read all those thoughts, I quickly formed something more coherent and less gushing to 'speak' directly to him.

I can't tell you how good it is to hear you, I thought-spoke. *Did Nico and Cal find you?*

Yes, they got away from the man with the knife. I'm with Nico now. We're coming to get you. I'm—

I'm not in the room any more, I thought-spoke quickly. *They locked me in a cupboard next door. I'm still in the basement, though. It's pitch black.*

Oh, Ketty. The sympathy in Ed's voice brought more tears bubbling into my eyes.

Please stay in my head, I thought-spoke, wiping my eyes.

I'm not going anywhere.

The strength in Ed's voice – and the concern – made me feel calmer. Ed had always had that effect on me. Solid and dependable, he was, truly, my best friend. We'd dated briefly, before Nico and I got together. And I sometimes wondered if Ed still liked me. But he never said anything about that directly.

I blushed, realising Ed would have been able to see those thoughts of mine, running along the surface of my mind. He always says that mind-reading is like swimming in the sea. You can stay on the surface or you can dive to the depths. Unless he's looking for something specific, Ed thinks it's unethical to go diving. But I wasn't even trying to hide the thoughts I'd just had.

Don't worry about it. Ed's voice in my head sounded emotional. *I'll just stay here in the background to let you know what's going on.*

Where are you now?

Just a few streets away. Hang on, we'll be there soon.

Reassured, I resumed my search for something to help me

break down the door or – if the two men who'd captured me came back – something I could use to defend myself. I made sure I thought clearly about what I was doing, so Ed would be able to see it on the surface of my thoughts.

Good idea, he thought-spoke.

I moved my hand slowly across the cold, dusty floor. I came to a small metal box. Feeling gingerly inside, I touched curved metal. Something small. I picked it up. It was a spanner. I couldn't see it properly, of course, but the shape was unmistakable. My trembling fingers felt beside it and found a screwdriver with a slim wooden handle and a long metal shaft. The metal felt rough. Rusty. It didn't matter. The slim shaft gave me an idea. I picked up the screwdriver and felt for the door. I found the handle and the lock and shoved the screwdriver inside. With a clang, the key inside the lock fell to the floor outside. Heart racing, I crouched down. There was a tiny gap under the door. I squeezed my fingertips underneath, all my focus on reaching the key.

Flashing lights. A sweet scent in my nostrils. Unbidden, I was falling into a vision.

The pain in my leg is worse. It sears right through me. My arms are flailing. I can't breathe. Beside myself. A blinding light explodes in my head. It shoots away from me, along a dark tunnel.

Ketty? Ed's voice in my head pierced through everything else. I came to with a rush. My hand was still under the door, outstretched, feeling for the key. As usual after a vision, my heart was racing and I was panting for breath. But how had

30

that vision happened? I hadn't seen into the future without intending to for weeks.

Are you okay, Ketty? Ed thought-spoke.

Yes. I tried to steady my breath. *I had a vision. I didn't mean to . . . it just happened.*

Was that what happened? It was weird . . . it felt like when people are asleep. Everything buried under the surface.

So you couldn't see what . . . what I saw?

No. Well, I might have done if I'd pushed harder, but no. Was it useful?

Not really, I admitted. I resumed my search for the key outside the door. I was just starting to think it had fallen too far away from the lock for me to reach, when my fingertips felt the rough, serrated indentations on its side. I clawed it towards me. There was still no sound from the men outside, but surely Broken Nose was still here somewhere. I held my breath, listening hard.

Nico and I are almost with you, Ketty, Ed thought-spoke. *Cal and Dylan are here too. They're keeping watch at the end of the road.*

I'm going to let myself out, I thought-spoke back.

Okay. Be careful.

Ed's presence in my head withdrew. I knew he was sitting back again, letting me focus on what I was doing.

My hand shook as I fitted the key in the lock. It was stiff to turn, but I managed it. I opened the door slowly. It gave a single squeak which sounded loud to my ears.

I held my breath, listening for sounds from above. But the

31

basement and the café upstairs were silent. I crept out into the gloomy corridor. I headed for the stairs. At least there was a little light out here, creeping in under the closed doors of the basement. Up the stairs, my eyes adjusted further. I stood at the top step, my hand on the door knob. There was still no sound from the café on the other side.

Where are you, Ed? I thought-spoke.

A few doors along. Less than thirty seconds away.

I hesitated. The others would be here any moment. Maybe I should just stay safe behind this door until they got here.

Yes, stay put, Ed urged.

No. If the two men were on the other side of this door, I would distract them by opening it. That would give Nico a better chance of disarming and defeating them.

I pushed the door softly open. It was stuck. I pushed harder. Something heavy was on the other side. Had they left it there on purpose in case I got out? No, surely not. Whatever it was shifted as I shoved at the door. With a final wrench, I opened it enough to see what was lying there. I gasped.

It was Broken Nose. He was on his back, blood seeping from a wound in his chest. I looked into his face. His eyes were open but blank. I'd seen it before . . . too many times to doubt what I was looking at.

This man was surely dead.

5: The Green Door

I looked up from Broken Nose's lifeless body as Nico and Ed rushed into the café. Nico had his arms outstretched, ready to perform telekinesis. He glanced from left to right, taking in Broken Nose on the floor by the basement door, then looking over to the bar. I followed his gaze. Knife Man was slumped against the counter. His head lolled to one side. Ed scuttled over and pressed his fingers against Knife Man's neck. He shook his head.

'I can't feel a pulse,' he said.

I stood up. None of us had yet spoken, but it struck me that we were all taking the situation in our stride. A few months ago coming across two dead bodies would have freaked all of us out. I wondered uneasily what it said about me that my main feeling right now was confusion.

Who had killed these men? And why?

'I see you didn't need us, Ketty,' Nico said drily. He grinned at me.

I gazed at the two bodies. Part of me wanted to smile back

33

but, again, I felt uneasy. Two people had died – and, okay, so they were bad guys who had tried to lock us up for reasons we didn't understand, but it seemed wrong to be making a joke that I could have done this.

Ed was searching Knife Man's pockets, over by the bar. I crouched down again and felt inside Broken Nose's jacket.

'What are you looking for?' Nico asked impatiently.

'Something that will explain who these men are, why they took us and why they've been killed.' Ed glanced over at me. 'Are you all right, Ketty?'

'Let's get out of here,' Nico insisted. 'Whoever killed these men could come back any moment.'

Ed nodded. 'Okay, just a sec.' He'd retrieved Knife Man's wallet and was looking through the various sections inside.

'Come on, Ed, we should go,' I said. 'Will you make remote contact with Cal and Dylan and tell them to meet us outside the green door on the far side of the church?'

'Why?' Ed got to his feet. 'What's so important about that door?'

'Ketty recognised it from her vision ...' Nico explained, '... eventually.'

I ignored this dig and we set off. Another time Ed might have asked more about my vision – and why Nico was being so mean – but, right now, he was preoccupied with the two men we were leaving behind.

'I wish we understood what those guys were after,' Ed said. 'Something about this whole set-up doesn't make sense.'

'We shouldn't get distracted,' Nico said. 'Whatever those men wanted with us, it doesn't matter now.'

'How do we work out what does or doesn't matter, Nico?' I said quietly.

Nico shook his head. He said nothing.

I bit my lip. Why was it so hard for me and Nico to communicate at the moment?

The road curved around slightly and Dylan and Cal came into view. They were already outside the green door of the church. Even from this distance I could see the massive look of relief on Cal's face as he caught sight of me. It struck me that Nico, despite supposedly being my actual boyfriend, hadn't yet bothered to check if I was properly okay. I mean, I know I'd only been separated from him for a few minutes in the end, but still ...

As we reached the green door, Cal pulled me into a big hug.

'Are you all right, Ketts?' he said, his voice full of emotion.

'I'm fine,' I said, hugging him back.

'Have you had any more visions about what's behind this door?' Dylan asked.

I hesitated, thinking about the cold passageway, the pain in my leg and the bright light. 'Yes, but nothing that really makes sense,' I said.

'I think Ketty should rest before we do anything else,' Ed said firmly. 'Cal needs to sleep too. He flew for hours and hours and—'

35

'I'm fine,' I said quickly.

'Me too,' Cal added.

Ed looked at Nico, appealing for support, but Nico shook his head.

'We need to keep going.' He held out his hands in front of the door. It was large and wooden, with brass rivets. Close to, it was obvious that not only was the green paint chipped and peeling, but the wood underneath was rotting as well. 'Before I open this door,' Nico went on, 'everyone needs to be prepared. We don't exactly know what's on the other side, but we have to assume it's something to do with the Medusix drug. This church looks run-down. It could be a meeting place, or even a production area where people come to work. We can't be too careful.'

'So what's your plan for when we're inside?' Cal asked.

Nico turned to me. 'Any chance of you seeing into the next few minutes for us?'

I stared at him. He *knew* how hard it was for me to have a vision when I felt tense and anxious. I'd just been shoved in a cupboard by two angry men who, in turn, had been brutally killed. These were not good conditions for me to foresee anything.

'No,' I muttered, my face burning. 'I'm too stressed to have a vision right now.'

Dylan rolled her eyes. It felt like the last straw.

'What's your problem, Dylan?' I snapped.

The atmosphere tensed. Nico looked at me, his face expressionless.

36

'Calm down, Ketty,' he said. 'It's fine that you can't have a vision. It just means we have to prepare for the worst ... Medusix is a secret, illegal drug. If there are people in here making it, there could easily be people in here guarding the operation.'

'Which means guns,' Ed said anxiously.

'Could we get on with this?' Dylan snapped.

'Fine, you should stand in front, Dylan,' Nico said. 'Protect us if we come under fire. Cal and I can deal with whoever attacks us. Then we'll let Ed through to mind-read whoever's there.' He turned to me. 'Maybe you could just concentrate on seeing into the future and not getting hurt.' He smiled, but it didn't seem amusing to me. What Nico was basically saying was that everyone else had a role to play using their Medusa ability, while I was going to be about as useful as a chocolate teapot.

That wasn't fair. I wasn't looking for special treatment but, if Nico was going to talk about everyone's skills, how come he didn't acknowledge that without my vision of the green door we wouldn't be here in the first place?

We all took our positions, Nico and Dylan in front. Nico twisted his hand. The large door groaned as the lock released. Dylan stepped forward and pushed it gently open. We all huddled behind her, making it easier for her to reach out with her arms and extend her protective force around us all.

Dylan walked through the doorway. Peering over her shoulder, I could make out a high-ceilinged church interior, with rows of wooden pews leading to a simple wooden altar at the far end. Dawn light shone in through the grubby windows, lighting the dust that floated in the air.

My heart pounded as we followed Dylan further inside. Where was the cold, damp passageway I'd seen after the door in my vision? I'd been skipping through time when I saw it … did the passageway belong to a different place? This church interior certainly didn't feel the same as anything in any of my visions.

'Maybe there's nothing relevant to Medusix in here,' Ed whispered.

I shook my head. That was the one reliable thing about the ability to see into the future. I rarely saw things that didn't turn out to be significant. And my vision had showed me the church door. Surely the church itself *must* be important?

'Let's take a look round,' Nico whispered.

'AAAGH!' A loud, high-pitched scream.

I jumped. The sound had come from a door at the far end of the church, beyond the altar.

Who on earth was there?

6: The Recruit

'Come on,' Nico ordered.

'Shouldn't we split up ... some of us hold back?' Cal asked. 'It could be a trap.'

'No.' Nico frowned. 'We have to stay together. We're stronger as a unit.' He strode off across the church. Ed and Dylan followed. Cal and I exchanged a glance. I knew, without either of us saying anything, that we were both slightly irritated by Nico's high-handed manner. I mean, staying together made sense to me as well, but he could at least have waited for us to agree before walking away.

The atmosphere was tense as we reached the door.

Dylan pushed past Nico. She tried the handle. The door wasn't locked. It opened slowly, creaking into the echoing silence of the church. A bead of sweat trickled down the back of my neck.

Beyond the door was a small, windowless room with a table, several chairs and a row of cassocks hanging from pegs along the wall. The only light came from a lantern perched on the table. As my eyes adjusted to the light, I caught sight of a shadowy figure huddled against the wall opposite.

'Hello?' I said.

'Hello.' The voice was a girl's. Young and nervous and with a strong accent.

She stepped into the light of the lantern. She was younger than us – about eleven or twelve I was guessing – with long dark hair and a grubby smudge on her button nose. I was guessing she was quite pretty under the dirt.

'I, Tania,' she said. She gulped.

I looked around. Ranged in a row as we were we must look really intimidating.

I stepped forward, smiling to put the girl at her ease.

'We heard you scream,' I said. 'Are you okay?'

Tania nodded.

'What on earth is going on?' Ed muttered.

'You'll have to mind-read her, Ed,' Dylan said, her voice full of suspicion.

'No,' I said. 'We can't just assume everyone we meet is untrustworthy.'

Dylan snorted.

'Anyway I don't think mind-reading would work with her, beyond general emotions,' Ed said. 'She doesn't sound like she thinks in English.'

'Mind-read?' Tania said.

She said it too casually. I was suddenly certain this was a trap.

'She knows what we can do,' I said, my anxieties mounting.

Behind us, the door slammed shut. A key turned in the lock. Nico immediately raised his hand.

'My telekinesis isn't working,' he said.

I looked at Tania. 'What's going on?'

Tania shook her head.

'Look!' Cal pointed to an air vent in the base of the wall beside the table. A thin tube poked out through its bars. As I saw it, I felt a fine mist clutch at my throat.

'It's Medutox,' I said.

Medutox. The drug we'd encountered for the first time just a couple of weeks ago, which had rendered all our psychic abilities useless.

Nico was twisting his hand – a classic telekinetic move. Except ... He turned to meet my eyes. His shocked expression said it all.

'I've lost my powers,' Ed gasped.

'Me too,' Dylan cried beside him.

I looked round frantically. There must be some other way out of the storeroom. But it was completely sealed. No doors or windows. I groaned. We couldn't have picked a worse place to escape from if we'd been trying.

The Medutox was still being pumped into the room. Cal tried to leap up, onto the table. But instead he just landed back on the ground with a dull thud.

'It's reached me too,' he said. 'I can't fly any more.'

I stared at the metal pipe, knowing that my own flaky

ability to see into the future must be gone too. Who was out there? Was it the man experimenting with Medusix? It must be, if he also had access to the counter-drug, Medutox.

'What do you know about the Medutox?' Dylan demanded angrily, turning on Tania.

'What about the Medusix?' Nico added, his fists clenched. 'Why are you here? Who sent you?'

Tania backed away.

'I am recruit,' she said. 'I join to get special powers.'

I stared at her. 'Recruit for what?' I asked.

'Join what?' Cal demanded.

And then the door opened. My hand flew to my mouth as a familiar face peered round the doorway.

It was Jack Linden – the man who had originally found us and brought us together. Linden had tried to take us and sell us to the highest bidder more than once before. His wolfish face creased with a smile, his bright blue eyes twinkling as he looked around the room.

'How nice to see you all,' he said smoothly.

'It's *you*?' Dylan sounded appalled. '*You're* the person who's been experimenting with Medusix?'

'No, my job was just to find you,' Jack said, still smiling as if we'd all just met up for a picnic.

'What d'you mean?' I said. 'Why?'

Jack ignored me. He entered the room properly.

Two men followed him inside. I stared at them. 'That's Knife Man and Broken Nose . . .' I breathed.

'How the hell are they here?' Nico demanded.

'They were *dead*,' Ed gasped.

'A trick,' Jack said. 'For some reason we don't understand, Medusix just makes adults unconscious for a few minutes – so they look like they're dead – then it passes, leaving no trace. The effect on children is different ...'

'What does it do to kids?' I asked. 'Does it give them psychic abilities?'

'Never mind that now.' Jack clicked his fingers and the two men headed straight for Nico and Dylan, handcuffs dangling from their hands.

Nico jumped back, still twisting his hands, desperately trying to make his telekinesis work. But it was no good. The Medutox had completely taken our powers away.

I sucked in my breath. This had *all* been a trap. Knife Man and Broken Nose had been working for Jack all along.

'How did you find us?' Nico asked as Broken Nose clamped his wrists with handcuffs.

'Technically *you* found *us*,' Jack said. 'Thanks to the stories you read about telekinesis in the area.'

'You mean those were made up?' Ed said, his face paling.

'No, the stories were true.'

'So someone really *was* performing telekinesis?' Nico demanded.

'So Medusix works?' Dylan asked.

'But you said it just made adults unconscious for a few minutes,' Ed added.

'Did you give the Medusix to children? Did it work on them?' I asked.

Jack batted away our questions with his hand. 'None of that matters right now.' He smiled at me. 'Anyway, once we knew you were coming, we relied on Ketty to do the rest.'

I looked at the dusty wooden floor. How humiliating. All my efforts to have a vision. And they'd just led us all into this trap.

'It's all worked out very well.' Jack grinned. 'I wasn't sure if the Medutox would work unless we got you in an airtight space.' His grin deepened. 'Wonderful stuff, Medutox.'

I looked over at Tania again. She was blushing, her expression a mix of pride that she'd played her part in trapping us and embarrassment that she'd tricked us. And there was something else too – a look of concern. What was that about?

'You did good, Tania.' Jack chuckled. 'Come on, we're going back to the castle.'

'How is Bradley?' Tania asked.

'Who?' I said.

Tania threw a glance in my direction. 'He takes the Medusix first. My turn next, but he is not well.'

'We can talk about that later,' Jack said. 'There's been a set-back.'

'What set-back?' Tania asked.

But Jack paid her no attention. He gave a signal and Knife Man strode over to me, drew a set of handcuffs from his pocket and fastened them around my wrists.

For the second time in less than an hour, I was a prisoner.

7: An Old Acquaintance

Jack bundled us into the back of a van that was parked outside the church. He locked the door. As soon as the van set off, everyone turned on Tania.

'What do you know about Medusix?'

'Who told you?'

'How did you find out?'

Cal, Nico and Dylan all spoke at once. The girl's eyes widened. She looked terrified.

'Okay, back off, everyone,' I insisted. Sometimes the others – especially Nico and Dylan – didn't realise how overwhelming they could be. And Tania, whatever part she'd played in trapping us, was still only a kid.

Dylan rolled her eyes, but all three of them quietened down. I turned back to Tania. 'Please don't be scared.' I spoke slowly and with a smile. 'We just want some answers.'

The girl nodded. 'Mr Jack came to me. Said he would make me special.'

I glanced at the others. This was a familiar story. Jack had introduced himself to all of us in much the same way, promising us the world if we would let him help us develop our Medusa gene powers.

'My name is Ketty,' I said. I introduced the others.

'Did Jack ... Mr Jack ... give you special pills or ... or a ...'

'Medusix,' Tania said. 'But not Mr Jack. Another man. He bring a drink of Medusix. But only Bradley drinking it so far.'

Cal let out a low whistle. 'So you haven't been given Medusix yet?' he said.

'No.' Tania's face scrunched into a worried frown. 'Only Bradley drink. Then he sick. Very sick.'

'That's because Mr Jack is a bad man,' I said. 'So is this other man.'

'You think?' Dylan snapped sarcastically.

'No.' Tania shook her head. 'It will all be good.'

'No, it won't,' I said. 'You can't trust Jack.'

Tania stared at me.

'Ketty's right,' Ed said. 'Jack's one of the bad guys.'

'Where is this other boy ... Bradley?' Nico asked.

'I ... I don't know.' Tania looked uncertainly from Nico to me.

The van turned a corner and we started bumping along a rough, ridged track.

'I don't understand how Jack laid this trap for us,' Ed said thoughtfully. 'I mean, he knew we would probably come to Lovistov, but how did he know exactly when we'd arrive?'

'Did anyone mention the fact that we were coming to anyone?' Nico glared round the truck.

'No, of course we didn't,' I said.

'Actually, I told Harry,' Dylan said, a defensive note in her voice.

We all stared at her. Harry Linden was Jack's son. There was no love lost between father and son, to be sure, but still I was shocked Dylan had taken such a risk.

She threw me a defiant look. 'There's no way Harry would have said anything. You know he doesn't even talk to his dad.'

This was true. Since being used by Jack to trick us earlier in the year, Harry had worked tirelessly to help us. He and Dylan were going out together too and Harry clearly adored her – a fact which frankly baffled the rest of us.

Ed shook his head. 'Jack could have hacked into Harry's phone. Harry wouldn't have needed to say anything.'

'Well done, Ed.' Jack's voice echoed out from the front of the truck. 'Got it in one.'

I froze. So did the others.

'He can hear us,' Ed whispered.

'You're a genius,' came Jack's reply.

'I told you Harry didn't say anything deliberately,' Dylan said.

'Sssh,' Nico ordered. We all lowered our voices.

'What are we going to do?' I whispered.

'Okay, listen. The Medutox will wear off after thirty minutes,' Nico hissed. 'We have to keep trying our powers.

Hopefully there'll be a few minutes when they don't realise we can use our abilities. That's when we have to act.'

'That's right,' Cal added quietly. 'When we get wherever we're going, look out for air vents, skylights ... places they might not think we can use. We don't know how much this Jack Linden knows about our skills.'

I looked at Ed. Dylan gave a low snort.

'Jack knows *everything* about our skills,' she said.

'Not mine,' Cal protested.

'I wouldn't be too sure of that,' I said. 'Jack's smart.'

'And ruthless,' Ed added.

'The important thing is that we stay together,' Nico whispered.

A few minutes later, the truck stopped and we got out. We were parked in front of a huge grey castle with a lake to one side and pine trees on the hill beyond. I looked round at the windswept landscape. There were no other buildings in view.

The area was completely deserted.

'Man, what a place.' Nico looked up at the turrets on top of the castle. It rose gloomily over us, an intimidating presence against a steel-grey sky.

Tania huddled next to me. I put my arm round her shoulder.

'We here before,' she whispered. 'Bradley here too.'

Jack and the two guards herded us inside. We stood in a hall, high-ceilinged and made of grey stone. It was virtually empty – no lights, no furniture. Our voices echoed around the cold, damp room.

'Why are we here?' Nico demanded.

'What are you going to do with us?' Dylan said. 'Is Harry here too? Is he okay?'

'Harry's not here but he's fine.' Jack gave her a charming smile. 'He'll be pleased to know you were asking, that's if I can ever get him to speak to me again.'

'How are you involved with Medusix?' I asked.

To my surprise, Jack stopped and turned to me. 'We're hoping to make it work. Now you're here, things should get easier.'

'What d'you mean "make it work"?' I said. I glanced at Tania, remembering what she'd said about the other boy, Bradley. He'd been given Medusix and was now sick. 'You got that boy to take it. Didn't it work with him? You said someone had been performing telekinesis earlier.'

'Ah,' Jack said. 'We've had some complications on that front. I told you that Medusix makes adults unconscious for a few mintues. Well, it knocks kids out too. The upside is that children show signs of psychic ability first. The downside is that they don't regain consciousness so easily.'

Tania gasped. 'So ... Bradley is *unconscious*.'

'Who is this "we" you keep referring to?' Nico added. 'Who else is involved?'

Jack raised his eyebrows. 'I can't tell you any more now, but please understand we have no plans to hurt you. We're just trying to work on the drug.'

'Are you going to experiment on us as well?' I asked.

'Of course not.' Jack looked surprised. 'We're going to learn from you.' He beckoned to the guards to lead us away.

At first I thought we were all being taken to the same room, but once we had gone through a couple of heavy wooden doors, Jack and Knife Man took Ed and Nico away. I opened my mouth to protest, but they were gone too fast, leaving Cal, Dylan, me and Tania with Broken Nose. He forced us down a steep flight of stone steps to a narrow corridor where we had to walk single file. Cal was in the lead. I could see his head darting this way and that, clearly looking for an escape route, but the walls looked a metre thick, and there were no windows whatsoever. After a minute or so of walking like this, down more steps and along another corridor, we reached a cell.

Broken Nose shoved us inside. Scowling, he took swabs from inside our mouths, plus a scraping of skin from our arms. Nothing that hurt. It took a few minutes, after which he locked the door and left.

The cell was just a few metres square. No furniture, no windows. A single lantern, complete with sputtering candle, stood beside the column that rose through the centre of the room. It cast spooky shadows around the room. It was still early morning outside, but down here it felt like the middle of the night.

Tania sank onto the cold stone floor. Tears were leaking out of her eyes.

'Bradley is really ill,' she wept. 'This is not what Mr Jack promised.'

I bit my lip, feeling sorry for her.

Dylan looked at her with far less sympathy. 'Well, that'll teach you,' she snapped.

'I wonder who Jack's working with,' Cal mused.

'It'll probably be a scientist,' I said. 'Jack knows a lot about IT, but he's no expert in genetics. Whoever is trying to make the Medusix work would need to be.' I paused. 'If only we knew what they were trying to do with it.'

Cal walked over and squatted down in front of Tania. 'Hey, that boy – Bradley – who was given the Medusix drug ... what did he do after he'd taken it? Anything ... odd? I mean, before he was taken ill?'

Tania looked over at me, confused.

'Odd? What kind of odd?'

I thought back to the news item Ed and I had found – about the car that seemed to moving telekinetically across the car park and the workman's tools dancing around each other.

'Could he move things?' I said. If we knew more precisely what the boy had done, we might be able to work out what Jack and this other man planned to do with us all. 'You know ... could the boy they gave the Medusix to move something without touching it?'

Tania stared at me as if I were mad.

'If we hadn't been sprayed, we could just show her,' Dylan said gloomily.

'We'd need Nico to demonstrate telekinesis,' I muttered.

'We don't need Nico,' Cal said. 'Pretend to move that lantern,

Ketty. I'll lift it up – normal style – to show Tania what we mean.'

'Go on, Ketty,' Dylan urged.

'Okay.' I shrugged. I couldn't really see how us acting out a bit of telekinesis was going to help, but I supposed anything that might prompt Tania to give us more information was worth a try.

Cal had picked up the lantern and stood out of sight behind the column.

'Ready,' he said.

'Okay.' I turned to Tania. 'Look at the lantern. Could the other boy do this?' I pointed my hand at the lamp then lifted my palm slightly, as I'd seen Nico do so many times. 'See, I'm not touching the lamp,' I said.

On cue, Cal – his hands out of sight – lifted the lantern into the air. From where we were sitting, it did look like the lantern was moving without support . . . that *I* was making it happen.

Tania frowned. 'You think other boy do this for real?'

'Yes,' Dylan said excitedly. 'Did you see him do something like that?'

'No.' Tania shook her head for emphasis. 'No, I never seen.'

Dylan sighed. 'Maybe they've been experimenting on this other boy separately.'

I nodded, feeling despondent. We were no closer to working out what was going on than before.

Across the room, Cal set the lantern carefully back down. I wandered over to him. The guards had taken our backpacks

52

before shoving us into this cell. All our food and drink were inside them and I was hungry and thirsty, as well as freezing cold.

'We have to get out of here,' I said.

'I know.' Cal moved closer to me. 'I've got an idea but ...' He hesitated. 'It'll mean all of us working together.'

'We can do that,' I said. 'What's the idea?'

'Attack Broken Nose when he comes back,' Cal said. 'I know it's obvious, but it's our only option. I can't see another way of getting past the locked door – once we're through, we just need to hide out for a bit then our powers will come back and I can fly us out of here.'

'What about Ed and Nico ... and this boy they've been using the Medusix on?' I said.

'I'll come back for them,' Cal said. 'I think we can do this ...' He moved nearer to me again. 'You know, you and I are good together, Ketty ...'

I was suddenly aware of just how close he was standing. I gulped. I liked Cal. I'd liked him as soon as I'd met him, but I didn't think of him in *that* way.

I wanted to move across the cell. After all, Broken Nose could come back any second. We needed to get the others ready. But there was something about Cal's presence that held me where I stood.

What about Nico? I said to myself. Truth was, right now I wasn't sure where things stood with Nico. He'd been distant and critical since we'd left the ranch in Australia. And before then I'd hated the way he'd pretended he liked

Amy, acting all flirty with her just because he liked the attention.

I looked up at Cal. He would never behave like that to get a girl to notice him. I mean, there was something a bit reckless about him ... a dangerous edge even, but he was definitely steadier than Nico. More ... dependable.

Cal was gazing down at me. He was still standing very close. I took a step back. Turned round. Dylan was watching us. She raised her eyebrows at me.

'What?' I said, more forcefully than I meant to. 'Cal has a plan. Listen.'

We beckoned Tania, then Cal went through the detail of what he thought we should do.

About two hours passed. Medutox was obviously being released into the room from somewhere, because none of our powers came back. I could feel the odourless mist on my face and clutching at the back of my throat.

We didn't talk much. I couldn't stop worrying about Nico and Ed – and whether Cal's plan would work. At last footsteps sounded along the stone corridor outside. I peered through the thick reinforced glass panel at the top of the door. Broken Nose was heading towards us. Cal leaped up, his body tensed for action.

'Get ready,' I hissed. 'This is it.'

8: The Lake

'Okay?' Cal whispered.

'Yes.' I glanced round. Dylan was, as arranged, lying curled up on the floor across the cell from the door. The lantern stood beside her, creating dark shadows across her face. Cal and I waited on either side of the door. Tania huddled behind Cal.

Broken Nose wouldn't be able to see us unless he came right into the room.

We had ripped the bottoms of our T-shirts off earlier. I held one of the strips of material in my hand. The footsteps grew close. Broken Nose was right outside the door. I could hear his wheezy breathing as he positioned the key in the lock.

Dylan gave a low moan.

'What is matter?' Broken Nose asked Dylan as the door creaked open.

Dylan bent over her stomach and groaned more loudly. 'Aaagh, it hurts.' Her right hand rested lightly on the lantern.

I held my breath.

'Where others?' Broken Nose was edging into the room now, his hand on his gun. He craned his neck trying to see into the dark corners on either side of the door, where Cal and I were hiding.

Dylan moaned again. 'Aaagh.' She sounded completely convincing.

Broken Nose looked around. He muttered something in his own language that I didn't understand. I pressed myself flat against the wall behind the door as Dylan, right on cue, smashed the lantern onto the ground.

The light went out. The room sank into darkness.

'HEY!' There was a note of panic in Broken Nose's roar. We had to shut him up. And take his gun.

'Now!' Cal yelled.

I rushed towards Broken Nose, just able to make out his outline in the dark room. I grabbed his arm. Wrenched it back.

Broken Nose yelled out, pushing me away. I clung on. Cal grabbed the man's other arm. Tania rushed to help me. Dylan jumped up. A moment later she and Cal had the man's arms behind his back and were tying them together.

'Shut him up,' Dylan ordered.

I reached up with my T-shirt strip and wound the cloth round his mouth. Broken Nose's yells were instantly muffled. Tania was clamped round one of his legs. Cal bent down and wound a third strip of material around his ankles.

Dylan pushed Broken Nose to the floor. 'Done,' she said, panting.

'Everyone okay?' My heart was beating fast.

'Awesome,' Cal said. 'Come on, let's get out of here.'

We ran through the open door and into the corridor. The stairs that led up to the ground floor were to our left. Voices drifted down towards us.

We turned right, away from the voices. We ran along the corridor. Around the corner. We passed a couple of windowless cells like the one we had been kept in. A few seconds later we arrived at the end of the corridor and a narrow set of stone steps that led down to the floor below.

'Come on,' Cal said.

'No.' Tania tugged at my arm. 'Way out upstairs.'

'Wait,' I said. 'Think about what Tania's saying. We won't get out if we go down these stairs. We're already in the basement. We need to be going up to the ground floor.'

Cal hesitated for a second. Then Dylan grabbed my arm.

'Listen!' she whispered.

The sound of footsteps filled the corridor we had just run along.

'Someone's coming,' Dylan whispered. 'We have to go down.'

She was right. We crept quickly down the narrow stone steps. It had been cold everywhere in the castle, but as we ventured through the darkness it seemed to get chillier. I still couldn't see much, but the wall beside the stairs was damp as well as cold. I pressed my hand against the moss-covered stone. Freezing air was blowing in from somewhere down here – and the smell of stagnant water.

57

I thought back to our arrival all those hours ago and the lake we'd seen beside the castle.

'We must be close to the water,' I whispered as we reached the bottom of the stairs.

A rough stone tunnel led away from the steps. Light glimmered in the distance. For a second, I was reminded of my earlier vision – but that had been a bright, blinding glare.

Cal was already running towards the light. Dylan followed quickly after him.

'Come on,' Dylan hissed over her shoulder.

I grabbed Tania's arm. As we raced after the others, a voice yelled out above our heads. Again, I didn't understand what was being said, but whoever was shouting sounded furious.

'They know we've got out,' I panted. 'Hurry!'

As we ran, the tunnel sloped down and the stones underfoot became damp and slippery. We had to slow down so as not to fall over. I could hear people – the guards – shouting, their footsteps pounding along the corridor above.

Up ahead, Cal careered around a corner and disappeared from view. Dylan followed. Tania and I sped around the corner after them, then skidded to a halt. I stared at the scene in front of me.

The stone path we'd been running along widened out slightly, then disappeared underwater. The tunnel itself ended a few metres away, where an iron fence – like a portcullis – rose up out of the water. Its top reached right up to the tunnel ceiling and it was bound on both sides by the tunnel walls.

Beyond it the lake stretched away into the distance.

'No wonder it was damp,' Dylan said.

I nodded, my heart drumming against my throat. The fence was constructed of narrow metal bars. The space between them was far too small to slip through.

There was no way to get past.

'We're trapped,' I said.

Dylan looked over her shoulder, back towards the tunnel we'd just run through. The guards' footsteps thundered down the stone steps.

'There has to be a way,' Cal said.

I looked round, desperate. Light reflected off the water, dancing over the damp, mossy walls. Across the tunnel an iron lever stuck out from the wall. I raced across the slippery stone. Grabbed the lever. Yanked it down.

With a rusty clank, the iron fence that blocked our exit shifted. The bars rose up, creaking as they disappeared into the stone ceiling overhead.

I looked down at the water level. The fence was rising up but the bars were not yet clear of the water surface. The guards were closing in, their footsteps echoing off the stone walls.

'Come on.' I seized Cal's arm. 'We'll have to swim under the fence.'

He looked at me. A moment passed. The guards' yells grew even nearer.

59

'She's right,' Dylan said. 'Take a deep breath first,' she ordered, then took one herself.

With a splash, she landed in the water. A second later Cal jumped in after her. They disappeared under the surface.

'Let's go!' I turned to Tania. She was backing away from the water's edge. 'No. I no swim.'

I stared at her. 'You'll be fine,' I said. 'Trust me.' I held out my hand. A beat passed. The guards were surely almost here.

Tania nodded. I gripped her arm and, together, we leaped into the water.

The shock of the cold wet made me gasp. The water was *freezing*. My clothes clamped to my body. Beside me Tania was thrashing about in a total panic, creating waves of icy water that splashed over my face. Out of the corner of my eye I could see a guard rushing round the corner.

'Stop it!' I yelled. I raised my hand and slapped Tania's face.

Tania instantly stopped moving.

'Breathe!' I commanded. I took a deep breath myself, then forced my head under the water, dragging Tania behind me. She didn't resist. Still gripping her arm, I dived down, towards the fence. The water was murky, but not particularly deep – just a few metres. The iron bars of the fence were clearly visible just ahead. There was a gap between the bottom of the fence and the ground – only about a metre or so, but enough room to swim under. Dylan was through. Cal was forcing his way under. As I swam towards them, the fence stopped rising.

I swam hard, dragging Tania behind me. Panic rose inside me again. Was she okay? I couldn't look round. I had to get us both under the fence and out of the water as soon as possible.

I was already running out of breath. I focused on the fence ahead. Cal was through now. And then the fence gave a judder. I felt the vibration through the water.

No. I watched, appalled, as the fence began to lower. It was only a metre off the ground, getting closer to it every second.

I swam even harder, hauling myself and Tania through the cold, gloomy water. The fence was coming down – steadily, surely. I reached it and grabbed the bars, pulling Tania through the water until she was level with me. Wide-eyed she grabbed the iron bars of the fence.

The gap between the bottom of the fence and the ground was just half a metre now. There was no sign of Cal or Dylan. My lungs burned inside me as I pointed to the rapidly closing gap underneath. I *had* to get Tania through.

I desperately needed to breathe. My lungs were bursting. The pressure inside me was unbearable. I shoved Tania under the fence. It was still coming down. Tania wriggled through, clawing her way beneath the bars. I followed, pushing her along. My body rose in the water slightly. I was almost out.

Aaagh. A searing pain drove through my leg. One of the descending iron bars had struck my left thigh.

Horror flooded through the pain. This was *it* ... the moment from my vision.

61

I wanted to scream but the need to breathe was more urgent. Tania was thrashing in the water beyond the fence. I had to reach her ... to help her ... but I couldn't move my leg where the bar had struck me. Darkness clouded my eyesight. *Come on.* I *had* to move, but my whole body was refusing to obey me. Panic swirled like a tornado inside me. There was no room to pass. The bars were almost down. Above me. On top of me. Trapping me. Panic filled me, a tearing fear. Darkness overwhelmed me. Then a bright light, shining at the end of a long dark tunnel. Blinding me. *This* was from my vision too. Wetness all around me. Seeping into me, into my lungs. Darkness. I couldn't move. Couldn't think.

Images flickered through my mind's eye. Mum and Dad watching TV ... my brother, Lex, handing me the little troll doll he'd won at a fair, a crooked smile on his face ... and then Nico, his dark eyes twinkling ...

Nico, I thought. And then the dark tunnel enveloped me and I let myself drift towards the light.

ED

9: Demonstration

The others disappeared down a flight of stone steps.

I pulled back from my guard. He pressed his knife into my ribs.

'Come on, Ed,' Jack Linden said. 'They'll be okay. We're going along here.' He pointed across the hallway.

I exchanged a swift glance with Nico. It was horrible not being able to communicate telepathically. I couldn't quite believe how much I missed it. Only a few months ago I'd hated my mind-reading ability.

Nico looked furious.

'We have to follow Jack. We don't have a choice,' I muttered, in case Nico was thinking of making some kind of mad run for it. That would be just the kind of thing Nico would do ... and without warning me first, either. And it would be pointless. Apart from Jack himself, there was also Knife Man walking right behind us.

'Fine,' Nico said bitterly.

We followed Jack across the cold stone floor. Even

though we were inside, my breath made a white mist in front of my face. Jack led us through a wooden door and up a flight of stairs. We were now in a passageway on the first floor. Through another door and, all of a sudden, the castle warmed up a little. A thick carpet softened the floor and the walls were covered with brocade wallpaper and oil paintings. Clearly we'd entered the inhabited part of the building.

'Who lives here?' I asked Jack.

'Yeah, and who are you working for?' Nico added.

Jack's head whipped round. 'What makes you think I'm working for anyone?'

'You're no scientist,' I said. 'And whoever's kidnapped us wants to use us to help develop Medusix. Though I don't understand how he thinks we can do that.'

Jack stared at me, his expression carefully blank.

'I thought he *had* developed Medusix anyway,' Nico went on. 'Tania said you'd given it to someone else . . . a boy you conned into coming here like her?'

Jack opened the door to a small room. It was furnished in the same style as the rest of the inhabited part of the castle, with heavy, dark-coloured wallpaper, bars at the windows and a thick carpet on the floor. The room contained a lot of furniture – bookcases, chintzy sofas, elegant wooden side tables, ornate lamps . . . If Nico had been in possession of his telekinetic abilities he could have hurled any or all of these things at Jack and Knife Man.

But Nico, like me, had lost his Medusa powers back in the church about twenty minutes ago. Once again, I felt their absence keenly – and not just because of the vulnerable situation we were in. When had being able to mind-read become such a vital part of who I was?

Jack ushered us inside the room. He sprayed us both in the face with Medutox.

'You haven't answered our questions,' Nico persisted. 'Who are you working for?'

'You'll find out later,' Jack said shortly. He walked over to the door. 'It won't be long.'

'What about the boy you gave the Medusix to?' I asked. 'Bradley, where is he? Is he still unconscious?'

Jack paused, his fingers curled round the door handle.

'As far as I know, yes, he's still unconscious,' he said. 'The Medusix worked for a bit, then ...' He shut the door. Nico and I were left alone.

'That's terrible,' I said, sinking into a chair. 'They've made that boy really ill.'

Nico paced across the room. 'It *is* terrible,' he said. 'And it means the Medusix doesn't work properly. Which explains why we're here.'

'No it doesn't.' I looked up at him. 'How is having access to us going to help? People have tried before, haven't they? Taken our blood and done tests and everything ... it's never made a difference before.'

'Well, maybe these people think they're onto something new,' Nico said darkly.

I closed my eyes and tried to access my mind-reading ability again. It was no good. 'Jack just sprayed us again,

67

which means the Medutox will wear off in about half an hour, won't it?' I said.

Nico nodded. 'We'll have to be ready to act as soon as it does,' he said.

'Suppose Jack comes back and sprays us again before then?' I asked.

Nico shook his head. 'I don't know.'

He sat down on the sofa opposite me. He looked as desolate as I'd ever seen him. I wanted to ask him how he was ... quite apart from the situation we now found ourselves in, things between him and Ketty were obviously not going well. I'd seen the scornful looks they'd been giving each other. But Nico didn't look like he wanted to talk about it.

About an hour passed. Knife Man appeared a couple of times, to spray us with Medutox. Eventually Jack returned.

'Okay, guys, let's go.' Jack brushed his sleek dark hair back off his wolfish face and smiled.

'Go where?' I asked.

'To do what?' Nico added.

'You're both going to give a live demonstration of your powers,' Jack said.

Nico rolled his eyes. 'You've just taken our powers away,' he said.

'As you well know,' Jack went on, unperturbed, 'the Medutox you have been sprayed with will wear off ...' he checked his watch, '... in about twenty minutes. Come on.'

Gagged and bound, with blindfolds over our eyes, Nico and I were taken downstairs again. The cold air whipped

68

across my face as I was shoved outside, then bundled onto the back seat of a large car. I could hear Nico's muffled shouts coming from the seat behind me as the car drove off.

My heart thudded in my chest. Where were we going? What was Jack going to make us do?

We drove fast and hard. Jack sprayed us during the journey with Medutox, then left us alone. We drove on for what felt like ages, though probably less time passed than I imagined. I kept trying to reach out using remote telepathy but my powers didn't return, so it couldn't have been thirty minutes yet since the last spray.

The road changed from bumpy to smooth and back to bumpy again. At last we stopped. I was dragged out of the car and set on my feet. My hands and feet were untied and I was pushed across uneven ground. The sun beat down on my face, brightening the dark blur of my blindfold. Dextrous hands picked at the tape across my mouth. Then Jack's voice spoke in my ear.

'Don't yell out when I take this off,' he instructed. Then he ripped the tape off.

Ow. 'Where are we?' I said, rubbing my mouth. 'Where's Nico?'

'I'm here,' Nico said beside me.

Jack removed my blindfold. We were standing in a field. Nico was on my left – his wrists still tied together. Knife Man stood in front of us. Like Jack, he was wearing sunglasses.

Another man, also in shades, stood beside Jack.

I looked at the open countryside all around us. The field we were standing in led to another and another. Beyond the fields I could just make out a copse of trees and a long black railway track, with mountains in the distance.

'What are we doing here?' Nico said.

'It's almost thirty minutes since you were sprayed with Medutox, Ed,' Jack said, ignoring Nico. 'You should be able to mind-read in a few seconds.' He paused.

I thought of Ketty back at the castle. Maybe Jack's calculations were wrong and my powers were already back. I focused as hard as I could, trying to reach Ketty with remote telepathy. Nothing happened.

'Who do you want me to mind-read?' I said.

Jack nodded at the man beside him. He was suntanned and old – at least sixty – with greying hair and dark, leathery skin.

'This is Mr Ripley,' Jack said. 'He's the one I want you to mind-read.'

'Why?'

'The man I'm working for needs more money for his research into the Medusa drug. Mr Ripley is a potential backer.'

'More money for research?' Nico said.

'Yes, so far we've only had limited results,' Jack said smoothly.

'By "limited results", you mean making that boy unconscious?' I said.

Jack shrugged his shoulders. 'Sadly, yes,' he said. 'No

70

one wanted that to happen. But sometimes when you take risks there are unforeseen consequences.'

I gritted my teeth. It was so typical of Jack Linden to make it sound like he wasn't responsible for the boy's state. 'If you mess around with illegal, untested drugs then it's not that surprising that people end up unconscious,' I said.

There was a tense silence.

'Perhaps we should get on with this.' Ripley raised his eyebrows. He spoke in clipped English, but I sensed it was not his first language. There was the trace of an accent underneath.

'Go on, Ed,' Jack said, a threatening note creeping into his voice. 'Remember Ketty and the others are still back at the castle.'

I hesitated, not wanting, now, to see if my powers had returned. This wasn't the first time someone had tried to force me to mind-read another person. It suddenly struck me that as long as I could communicate telepathically, someone somewhere was always going to want to use my ability for their own ends. Which meant I would never be safe.

And neither would the people I loved. No, for the rest of my life they were going to live with this risk ... that someone might take them and use them to force me into action, as Jack was doing right now – with Ketty and Cal and Dylan.

'Hurry up, Ed,' Jack ordered.

In that moment I wished, more than anything, that I couldn't mind-read. I would have given anything to have been able to stop right then and there.

But that wasn't possible. As I looked into Ripley's eyes, I felt my telepathic ability surge back, like a feeling of readiness in my mind. A second later I was inside the man's mind. He was tense. I could feel the high level of anticipation of his thoughts: *What will this feel like? How will I know what this boy can see?*

I can just see surface thoughts right now, I thought-spoke. *Like you wondering how it will feel.*

The man gave a gasp. Inside his mind, I could feel the levels of shock and fear rising. This was a normal reaction in my experience. I guess it's pretty weird, finding someone else inside your head. But this man was also hugely excited, as if he was finally seeing the proof of some long-awaited experiment.

You're speaking to me without talking, he thought-spoke.

You're a genius, I thought-spoke back, remembering what Jack had said to me in the car earlier and trying to get a Nico-style edge of sarcasm into my voice. *What do you want me to do?*

Read my thoughts, he thought-spoke. *See if you can see what I want you and your friend to do next.*

I could feel him brace himself. I sighed. Tracking the thoughts people are trying to hide is actually one of the easiest aspects of mind-reading. It's obvious really. I mean, if you tell yourself not to think about something, you're already thinking about it. It's impossible to be aware of something and also not aware of it at the same time.

I waited a few seconds, letting the man focus on repressing his thought. *There.* I could sense the command to stop thinking about something and caught hold of it – a sensation like catching the end of a piece of string.

Now all I had to do was follow the 'string' and see what thought it led to.

No problem. Seconds later I saw into the man's mind.

I couldn't believe it.

I broke the connection.

'We can't do that,' I said. 'People will die.'

10: The Train

The man I'd been mind-reading laughed. I turned from him to Jack.

'We won't do it,' I said, feeling desperate. I had to warn someone ... find some way to stop it from happening.

As if reading my thoughts himself, Jack raised his hand and sprayed me and Nico with Medutox again. My mind-reading abilities were gone.

'What is it, Ed?' Nico asked.

'They want us ... you ... to make a train crash using telekinesis,' I stammered. I could, still, hardly believe it. 'It's a passenger train. Lots of people on board.'

'What?' Nico said.

'Why?' I turned to Jack. My heart was pounding. 'Why do you want to smash up a train and kill loads of innocent people?'

'There's someone on board Mr Ripley wants rid of,' Jack explained, adjusting his sunglasses with a finger. 'If the train crashes, it will look like an accident. It will also be a wonderful demonstration of Nico's telekinetic powers for Mr Ripley here.'

'I'm not using my telekinesis to make a train crash,' Nico spluttered.

'There will be consequences if you don't,' Jack said softly. 'Fatal consequences.'

I closed my eyes and thought of Ketty and Dylan and Cal, still trapped back at the castle with Tania.

'You're saying that if we don't help you, you'll kill the others ... my brother, my cousin and my girlfriend?' Nico said.

Jack smiled. 'You see how well we understand each other?' He paused. 'Although I'm surprised Ketty is still your girlfriend. I saw the way she and Cal looked at each other earlier. I think you've got competition there, mate.'

Nico curled his lip. For a second, I thought he was about to leap forward and headbutt Jack.

'Over here,' Jack ordered, pointing to the corner of the field closest to the trees. Knife Man held Nico and me by the arms as we walked over. As we neared the trees, the railway track I'd noticed before came into clearer view. It ran across the distant fields, curving in a bend across a flat stretch of ground. About five hundred metres on, the mountain range started and the track ran parallel with it for a while, before veering off again, into the distance.

'In another thirty minutes the train will be here. I timed your most recent doses of Medutox to wear off just before it arrives. At that point you, Nico, will use your telekinesis skills to force the train into the side of the mountain. Ed has already demonstrated his considerable powers. Now it's your turn.'

Nico said something extremely rude to Jack. Knife Man cuffed him round the head.

I stared across the low, flat fields, my eyes straining into the distance. There was no sign of the train yet. At least we still had thirty minutes to work out how to avoid making this train crash happen. I stared at the track. It ran on into the distance, as far as the eye could see. Jack pointed to a branch line that led off from the main track and ran downhill towards the mountains just a few hundred metres beyond.

'You have to turn the train onto that track, Nico,' he said. 'Smash it into the side of the mountain.'

My heart sank as I stared at the track. Our situation was hopeless. If Nico crashed the train, all the passengers would end up dead or maimed. If he refused, Ketty and the others would be the ones to die.

I looked sideways at Nico. His face was pale under the blindfold. I was sure he was running over the same options as I was.

'We'll work this out,' I said.

Nico's head jerked up. 'Yes,' he said, looking straight at me. 'Somehow we will.'

'You'll both do what you're told,' Jack snapped.

Time passed slowly. No one spoke. Every few seconds I tried remote telepathy, but it was no good. The Medutox was totally effective. Trust Jack. His great strength had always been that he fully understood just how powerful – and how limited – our abilities were. He was still wearing those sunglasses, his way of protecting himself from my mind-reading.

Not that I could mind-read right now. Surely my powers would return any moment. I *had* to reach Ketty. Warn her about what was happening. I took a deep breath and let it out slowly. The calmer I was, the easier it was for me to perform remote telepathy. I tried again. Still nothing.

'It's time.' Jack looked into the distance. I followed his gaze. A train was speeding across the track. It was just a hundred metres or so from the turn onto the branch line. 'Nico, your powers must be back by now?' Jack looked at him expectantly.

Nico pressed his lips together, refusing to answer.

'Nico?'

'Fine, they're back.' Nico turned to me, his expression desperate. 'Anything, Ed?' he said.

I knew he was asking about *my* Medusa power. 'Any second,' I said shortly.

Jack pointed at the train. 'Okay, Nico, get ready to turn that train down the hill.'

'And then crash it into the mountain?' Nico asked. On the surface he sounded angry, but I could hear the fear underneath his bravado.

'If you don't, Cal and Dylan and Ketty will die,' Jack said.

Nico glanced at me. 'This totally sucks,' he said.

77

'I know.' I met his gaze. It's kind of weird . . . Nico and I have never exactly been the best of friends but in that moment I'd never felt closer to anyone. Though I wasn't reading his mind, I knew exactly how he was feeling: that combination of frustration, fury and fear that takes you over when somebody is forcing you to do one bad thing to stop another bad thing from happening.

The train got nearer the bend in the track.

'I won't do it,' Nico said defiantly.

Jack signalled to Knife Man who brought his weapon up and pressed it against my neck. I gasped.

Nico's eyes widened.

'Don't make me give the order to have Ed killed in front of you,' Jack said.

I held my breath. Nico blinked rapidly. He turned away and focused on the train. As he did so, I realised that my telepathic powers were back.

I zoomed into Nico's mind. *Do what he tells you*, I thought-spoke. *Not for me, for the others.*

I want to, but how can I crash that train? It's totally wrong.

Please, Nico. We'll think of something before it hits the mountain.

Nico gave no sign that we'd just been communicating through telepathy but all of a sudden the train slowed down.

'What are you doing?' Jack barked.

Ripley stared on, his mouth open in wonder.

'I have to slow the train to make it turn properly,' Nico said through gritted teeth.

I smiled to myself, sure Nico was just trying to buy some time.

We all watched as Nico turned the train telekinetically. It curved round onto the grassy hill, still moving slowly. But, as it straightened out, it picked up speed. Why was Nico letting it move so fast? The mountain was now directly ahead of it – just a few hundred metres in the distance. The collision was surely just a few minutes away.

Slow it down, I thought-spoke. At that moment, Jack's radio buzzed. I broke the connection with Nico in order to concentrate on what Jack was being told.

The voice on the other end – one of the guards – spoke in broken English and with lots of static on the line. I could only just make out what he said.

'They've got out of the cell. All four kids.'

Yes. Dylan, Cal, Ketty and Tania were escaping!

Jack and Ripley exchanged looks. Ripley swore.

'Deal with it,' Jack barked into the radio. Then he switched off the call.

I stood for a second, taking in what I'd heard. If the others were making a run for it, maybe Nico didn't have to crash the train. I glanced over. The train was careering down the hill. If anything, it was going even faster than before.

I dived back into Nico's mind. *Nico, did you hear that? You can stop the train. The others are escaping.*

I can't stop it, Nico thought-spoke back, his voice full

79

of anxiety. *It's going too fast downhill – and it's too far away.*

What about the driver?

He must have panicked. I just saw him jump out of the driver's cab, Nico thought-spoke. You *have to stop the train. Stop it then get away.*

What? Me stop it? What was he talking about? *How?*

Like this.

Without warning, my legs lifted off the ground. I opened my mouth to scream as I soared into the air. The scream died in my mouth as I rose up into the sky. Nico was doing this. He was moving me using telekinesis. Jack and Ripley and Knife Man were all yelling at him. Their shouts faded as I zoomed away … as Nico teleported me across the field. With a terrible jolt, I realised I was heading for the speeding train. It was getting closer.

I flew through the air. 'Aaagh!' I yelled. I'd totally lost the connection with Nico. What was he thinking? I couldn't process it. I was too shocked. I mean, I'd been teleported by Nico before but never without warning – or at such high speed.

I tried to focus. To get back inside Nico's head.

What are you doing? I yelled in thought-speech.

I'm putting you on the train, Nico thought-spoke.

I looked down. The train was, indeed, looming up beneath me.

Suddenly Nico plunged me downwards. *Get ready to land*, he urged.

No, I can't.

You have to. Land and stop it crashing. Then get away. Get help.

But it's moving, I shrieked.

The train zoomed up. It was right there, just two metres below me.

One metre.

Stop the crash, Nico thought-spoke. *Get to safety. Get help.*

I braced myself. *Wham!* I landed with a thud on the top of the train. I lay spread-eagled for a long, terrifying second, and then I felt Nico release me, the force of the wind take me and – *no* – my body slid across the roof. Down I slipped. Down.

I flailed for a handhold. But the roof was hot, smooth metal.

I was on the edge of the roof. About to fall.

Falling.

11: The Crash

Hands flailing, I grabbed at the ridge that ran along the edge of the train roof. My legs were off the roof completely, dangling in mid-air. The train was running downhill – steep and fast. My eyes watered as the air rushed into my face.

Nico! My thought-speech was a scream.

Got you.

As Nico's words registered in my head, I felt a force against my body, pushing me back onto the roof of the train. I lifted one hand from the roof ridge and placed it on the smoother metal beyond. With a grunt, I brought my legs round so they were on the roof too. I could feel Nico's telekinesis, trying to hold me in position. I crawled a little further, until I was in the centre of the train roof. I lay panting, my cheek against the hot metal.

I was sweating and shivering all over.

Get up, Ed. Hurry!

What was Nico shrieking about now? For a second, I felt

a flicker of annoyance. I'd almost been flung off a train to my death; the least I needed was a moment to recover.

And then I remembered where the train was heading.

I looked up. The mountain loomed ahead, a massive expanse of thick grey rock – huge and lethal. The train full of people was careering towards it at top speed and Nico was unable to do anything to stop the crash. It was up to me.

I inched forward on the roof. I was right at the end of the carriage. There was just one more before the driver's cab at the very front. Nico was still holding me on the train, using telekinesis. I could feel the force of his energy, pushing me down, counteracting the force of the wind which was pushing me up and back. I reached out and grabbed the raised iron bars in front of me. I peered over the end of the carriage. The iron bars were actually the top of a set of metal steps that led down the back of the carriage. Clinging onto the bars, I eased myself around and found the steps with my feet. As I crept down the steps into the shelter of the carriage in front, the wind dropped. For the first time since I'd been flung into the air, I took a breath.

Nico? I thought-spoke, desperate to reach him. *Are you sure you can't stop this thing?*

Yes, I'm sure. Nico's thought-speech was a yell. *The driver's cab is open, though. You need to get into it and put the brakes on.*

What? He surely couldn't be serious?

I've done what I can. You're the only person who can stop

83

the train now, Nico thought-spoke. *They're about to spray me with Med—*

The telepathic connection between us disappeared – I could only remote mind-read others with full Medusa powers and Nico's telekinesis had clearly been taken away from him. This meant I was no longer being 'held' against the train. If I'd still been on the roof, the shock might have toppled me right off it but – as it was – I was clinging to the steps that led down the back of the carriage. I tightened my grip. The train was still hurtling downhill towards the mountain. I looked across the coupling to the carriage that lay between me and the driver's cab. A set of steps led up to the roof, just like the ones I'd just climbed down to get to the driver's cab. I was going to have to cross the coupling, climb up onto the roof of the next carriage and down the other end.

What's more, I had to do it right now.

Trembling all over, I balanced on the bottom step. I took one hand off the rungs behind me. The hill the train was speeding down was a blur on either side of me. I focused on the carriage in front. Sweat beaded on the back of my neck.

With a yell, I threw myself across the divide between the two carriages. I lunged for the steps on the other side. *There.* I gripped the rungs. The metal felt clammy under my sweating hands. My heart pounded in my ears. *No time.*

I reached up to the rung above, finding a foothold on the bottom step as I did so. Up I climbed, hand over hand. Seconds later I was at the top. I inched onto the roof of the train. Nico was, of course, no longer holding me in place but I was used to the train's motion now. It took an effort, but slowly I crawled forward along the roof. The mountain was looming ever closer. How far away was it? Less than two hundred metres I was guessing. Which gave me just a few minutes to reach the front of the train and apply the brakes. As I made my way, commando-style, across the roof, I could hear screams from the passengers inside. I speeded up.

Come on. A few moments later I reached the end of the carriage. I swung myself round. Down the steps. The driver's cab was opposite the coupling. The door at the back swung open, banging against the side of the cab. Inside it was empty.

I steadied myself, waiting for the open door ahead to swing completely open. *There.* I jumped across the coupling. Into the cab. I landed in a heap on the floor. My arm hurt. My whole body was bruised. My heart was thundering in my ears. I scrambled to my feet. Looked up. The mountain was just metres away.

I looked down. Desperate. Where were the brakes? The display of knobs and electrical controls in front of me was bewildering. I had no idea what to touch ... what to do ... I glanced sideways. A huge lever stuck out from the panel to my left. I grabbed it. Yanked it back. The train let out a screech. *No.* It was going faster.

I pushed it in the opposite direction, bracing myself against the side of the cab.

With a groan, the train slowed. *Yes.* I looked up again.

The mountain was almost here. I clung to the lever, forcing it down as far as it would go. The train was still slowing. But not fast enough.

'STOP!' I pushed at the lever again.

The train grew slower. Slower. The mountain right in front. Just metres away. It was terrible. Heart-stopping.

'AAAGH!' The lever was flat down, the train's gears grinding.

The mountain was so close I could see the ridges on the rock face.

I pressed down on the lever, closed my eyes and waited for the crash.

12: Escape

With a final groan, the train stopped. I opened my eyes. The mountain was centimetres in front of the driver's cab – less than half a metre from where I stood. I stared at the rock as the realisation of just how close the train – and I – had come to crashing into it sank in.

My legs trembled and I sank to the floor of the cab. I felt utterly exhausted. My body was drenched in sweat and my heart was still pounding. Behind me, I could hear the doors of the train carriages open. People were spilling out onto the field, shouting and yelling in a language I didn't understand. The relief in their voices, however, was unmistakable.

I closed my eyes and took a few deep breaths. I'd made it.

But there was no time to rest. Jack, Ripley and Knife Man were close by. I had to get away from here now ... find my way back to civilisation and alert the authorities.

At least I had my telepathic ability back. I sat up, trying to ease the trembling in my limbs. It was hard to focus on mind-reading. My brain was skipping about, refusing to relax enough to make remote contact.

I got to my feet, taking deep, calming breaths. I reached out for Nico. But his mind was still unavailable to me. I tried to make contact with Ketty. Nothing. I tried Cal, then Dylan. Still nothing. Had their escape attempt been foiled? Or were they free, just under the control of the Medutox for another few minutes?

It was possible that all four of them were still captives. Or worse.

I swallowed hard. Well, that meant getting help was down to me. I couldn't let them down. As I staggered to the door of the train driver's cab, I remembered Amy – my sister back in Sydney. As soon as I thought of her, I made contact.

Amy? I could feel her mind, slow and sluggish, coming to an awareness I was there. *Amy? It's Ed!*

Ed? Amy's thought-speech sounded bewildered. *Are you all right?*

Yes, Amy, listen. We're in a place just outside Lovistov in Kima. I've got away but the others are ... at least they might be ... prisoners.

Oh my gosh. Oh my gosh. Amy's thought-speech had suddenly gone from nought to sixty miles an hour. *Are you all right?*

I'm fine. Did you hear what I said? Jack Linden is here too, but he's working for someone. They're developing the drug. The Medusix. It's definite. We—

Slow down, Ed, Amy's thought-speech interrupted. *Where are you again?*

Lovistov. There's a castle not far outside the town. We're near that right now. There was a train. I hesitated, trying to collect my thoughts. *The others are trying to escape. But Nico is with Jack.*

The others are on a train? Amy sounded confused.

No. I peered outside the driver's cab. People were milling about ... hundreds of them, mostly still shrieking their heads off. I jumped down and joined them. Everyone was talking, some on their mobile phones. No one took any notice of me.

My legs were still shaky and my throat unbearably dry. The sun was high in a clear blue sky. It beat down, its heat fierce on my face. I peered into the distance. I could just make out the line of trees where we'd all been standing when Nico teleported me onto the train. The chances were high that Jack, Ripley and Knife Man had got back in their cars and were already on their way. I had to get out of here.

Ed? Amy's voice sounded in my head again. *What's going on?*

Jack Linden and another man I don't know captured us, I thought-spoke. *I've got away but I don't know about the others. Tell Dad. And Fergus Fox. I'm going to go now ... it's a castle near Lovistov. Tell them, Amy.*

Okay, but Ed, oh my gosh, will you contact me again soon?

Sure. I broke the connection with my sister and looked around again. Two young men were deep in conversation beside me. One of them had dropped his backpack. It was open at his feet, a bottle of water peeking out of the top. Beside the water I could just make out the edge of a black leather wallet.

I swallowed. I was desperately thirsty and I couldn't see how I was going to get away from here without money. And yet it was impossible to steal the wallet. It was terrifying to imagine doing it, not to mention completely immoral.

I looked across the crowd. No one had noticed me so far. Maybe there was another way. And then I gazed into the distance again and my heart skipped a beat. Two large cars were hurtling down the hill towards the train.

That had to be Jack and the others.

If they found me here, I'd be recaptured.

That settled it. Without thinking about it any further, I bent down. I grabbed the water bottle in one hand and the wallet in the other. I stood up, turned swiftly and walked away from the two young men, still deep in conversation. My shirt clung to my back, damp with sweat, as I forced myself to keep going. I mustn't look back.

I reached the gap between the train carriages that I'd leaped over earlier. I glanced across the fields again. The two cars were just a few hundred metres away. They'd be here within minutes.

Time to go. I scrambled across the coupling that linked the two carriages. Loads of people were milling about on this side of the train too, but I couldn't see the two cars any more. That was good. That meant they couldn't see me either. I took a gulp of water from the bottle and slid the man's wallet into my pocket. I'd check it out later. Right now I needed to get away from the train. A small wooded area marked the edge of the field we were in. Breaking into a run, I headed for it as fast as my still shaky legs could carry me. I didn't look over my shoulder until I reached the first tree. As I ducked behind it, I glanced round. No one was watching me, except for one little girl clutching a teddy bear. I leaned against the trunk, catching my breath. Then I set off again, darting through the trees to where the land opened out on the other side.

I was on the edge of another field. Beyond it was a road. *There.* I would head for the road. With any luck I'd be able to pick up a lift to a nearby town. I pulled the wallet I'd stolen out of my pocket. It contained a student ID card, and a few notes – I didn't understand the currency any more than I did the language, so I had no idea how much the money was worth.

I felt a stab of guilt. The owner was a student, which meant that he probably wasn't well off. Why couldn't I have robbed someone rich? Something bulky was tucked into the side of the wallet. I drew it out. A slim silver lighter. I slid the lighter and the wallet back into my pocket. As I did so, I promised myself I would get both of them back to their owner when this was over.

I took a final glance around. I was absolutely alone. I took a step out into the field, away from the trees. A twig snapped to my right. I darted back, behind the cover of the tree I'd just walked away from.

Another twig snapped. Someone was definitely here. Had they followed me from the train?

I held my breath, then peered round the tree trunk. The footsteps were crashing towards me now. My heart started pounding again. I tensed, my whole body alert, ready for danger.

'Ed?' The voice was a hoarse whisper, but as familiar to me as my own.

I stepped out from the trees as he came into view. He was stumbling towards me, the side of his face livid with a purple-red bruise, clutching his side.

Nico.

I opened my mouth to speak his name, but before I could say anything he slumped down, onto the ground. I rushed over.

'Nico?' I hissed. 'Nico?'

But his eyes stayed closed. He was unconscious.

13: The Return

My heart in my mouth, I shook Nico by the shoulder. He moaned, but his eyes stayed shut.

My heart was beating like it was about to explode. What on earth was I going to do if he didn't come round? Jack and Ripley and Knife Man couldn't be far behind him.

I shook Nico again. 'Wake up!' I yelled.

Nico opened his eyes. His focus was glazed. I looked at the terrible bruise on his face. Nico shook his head.

'I'm okay,' he said, his voice barely audible.

'What happened to your face?'

'Knife Man hit me,' Nico said. He was clearly struggling to keep his eyes open. 'But that's not why I passed out. Jack gave me a sleeping pill ... left me in the car. That's when I saw you by the train.' He offered me a weak smile. 'Hey, you did it, you stopped the train.'

I shoved my hands under his arms and hauled him upright.

'You can't give in and go to sleep,' I urged. 'We have to get out of here!'

'Okay ... okay ...' Nico opened his bleary eyes. He leaned against the nearest tree trunk to steady himself, then blinked. 'Which way?'

I pointed across the field to the road. 'Over there. We can flag down a car.'

Nico nodded. He leaned against me and we set off. It wasn't easy. I was taking most of Nico's weight as he walked, half dragging him across the field. I kept glancing over my shoulder but there was no sign of Jack or the others. As I forced Nico on, my mind went to Ketty. Surely, if she and the others had escaped, they would be free of the effects of the Medutox by now.

I focused on trying to reach her with remote telepathy, but Ketty's mind was in darkness. Presumably she was asleep, which seemed strange seeing it was the middle of the day.

I probed a little further. Sleep is a weird state to watch someone's mind in. Everything goes very still on the surface of the brain, though there are still thoughts and feelings expressed by the unconscious mind buried underneath.

That wasn't how it was with Ketty's mind right now. In fact, if I hadn't specifically thought about her and focused on reaching her, I wouldn't have known it was Ketty's mind I was inside at all. Was she unconscious? There was definitely a difference between the total pitch black of her brain in this state and the darkness – with glimmers of light sparking up from the unconscious – that characterised most people's sleeping brains.

I forced myself to disconnect and looked around the field again. Still no sign of anyone following us. Nico was leaning on me heavily, but at least his eyes were open.

'Hey, Ed, seriously you were amazing. Awesome. You saved everyone's lives.'

I could feel my face reddening. I hate to admit it, but Nico's praise has always given me a boost. I don't know why he has that effect on people, but it's not just me. Almost everyone he meets wants to impress him.

We were almost at the road. I could see a car in the distance. If we got a move on, we might be in time to flag it down. I forced Nico on. We reached the road a moment later. I held out my arm, hoping to stop the car, but it just sailed past us.

I bit my lip and took shelter in the trees that lined the road. Nico sank, gratefully, against a tree trunk.

'Don't worry, I'll get us another ride,' I said.

Nico looked up. 'Where to?'

'It doesn't matter,' I said, looking along the deserted road. 'We just need to get away from here. Then we'll figure the rest out.'

Nico nodded. 'Thanks, Ed.'

I stood, waiting for another car to pass. There was no sign of any traffic at all. I felt jittery. We *had* to get out of here as soon as possible.

As I waited, my mind went back to Ketty. Why hadn't I been able to reach her? I tried again, but her whole consciousness was still in darkness. Feeling troubled, I attempted to reach Dylan. Never my first choice for remote telepathy, thanks to her being so prickly, but at least she might know what was going on.

Dylan? I knew something was wrong as soon as I made contact. Whereas Ketty's mind had been dark and still, Dylan's was uncharacteristically chaotic. Normally her mind is highly controlled. Dylan doesn't like letting people in close ... or showing that she's vulnerable. But right now her thoughts and feelings were tumbling over each other, completely hysterical.

Dylan?

Oh, Ed. Dylan's thought-speech sounded almost tearful.

I tensed. This was really unlike her. I was itching to dive in and try and work out what she was thinking. I could sense Ketty was a big part of it. But mind-reading without per-mission is unethical. I try not to do it unless I have to.

What's happened? I thought-spoke

Ed, I'm so sorry ...

Was she *crying*? I'd never been inside someone's head while they were weeping before. It was like waves of misery washing over all Dylan's thoughts – drowning some ... bringing others to the surface ...

A thousand tiny hurts and losses, all bobbing about like debris from a shipwreck. And then the central thought – the heart of her misery – whirled up from the chaos and I saw exactly what was making Dylan cry.

Ketty didn't make it.

What do you mean? I thought-spoke. Panic rose inside me. *Where is she?*

I could feel the sobs racking Dylan from the depths of her being.

We tried to escape by swimming under a fence, into the lake. Cal and I made it out with Tania, but Ketty got trapped. Cal went back to try and rescue her but she was unconscious and he couldn't move her and the guards were swimming towards them so he ... he had to swim away.

I couldn't take it in. What was she saying?

We got to the shore, Dylan went on. *We're hiding out in this little farmhouse on the other side of the lake. But ... but not Ketty ... she's ... gone ... in the water ...*

I was still too stunned to formulate a single coherent thought.

Ed ... where are you? Are you all right? What about Nico?

Dylan's questions brought me back to the present. I suddenly realised another car had almost reached us. Nico was still lolling against his tree trunk, eyes closed. I looked up, my head still spinning with Dylan's news.

And then the car stopped. The door opened. In that instant I realised it was Jack's car and the man leaping out was Knife Man. Too late, I turned away. But Knife Man was already lunging after me, Medutox spray in his outstretched hand.

I felt the fine mist clutch at the back of my throat. The connection with Dylan was gone.

In that moment what she'd told me sank in.

Ketty was dead. That was why I'd only felt darkness in

her mind when I tried to contact her remotely. She had drowned in the lake. Alone.

I fell to my knees, overcome with terrible, consuming loss. I was moaning, barely aware when Jack rushed up and grabbed my arms, pinning my wrists behind me. Who cared what happened now?

My best friend in all the world was dead.

Jack shouted at me for about two minutes solid. I didn't take in a word of it. At last he stopped and let Knife Man drag Nico and me up to our feet. As we were bundled into the back of the car, Nico turned to me.

'What's going on?' he said, clearly forcing himself to speak through his drugged state.

I stared at him.

'It's Ketty,' I said, keeping my voice very low, so Jack and the others in the front of the car wouldn't hear.

Nico's eyes widened and I felt the horror of the loss all over again. I couldn't bear talking about it, but I had to tell him. I leaned forward and whispered in his ear what Dylan had just told me.

'So . . . so . . . Dylan says she drowned,' I finished.

Nico just stared at me. He blinked rapidly, as if he couldn't take in what I was saying.

'And now they've sprayed me again and the connection with Dylan has gone,' I stammered. 'But it doesn't matter,' I said, close to tears. 'Nothing matters any more.'

I drew back. Nico turned away. I didn't know what to say to him. There wasn't anything to say. A second later Knife

Man bound and gagged us. I sat back, numb, as we drove the rest of the way to the castle in shocked silence.

Jack left the gags on when we arrived, but he unbound our hands and feet so we could walk back to our room in the castle. After shouting at us when he recaptured us, he was now treating us with contemptuous disdain. When we reached the room, he sprayed us again with Medutox and left, locking the door behind him.

I didn't care what he did. I didn't even care we were prisoners again. All I cared about was Ketty. And she was gone.

As soon as Jack walked out of the room, I tore off my gag and slumped onto one of the brocade sofas, my head in my hands. Nico sat opposite me. Since we'd arrived back at the castle he'd lost the bleary look in his eye. Whatever Jack had given him was obviously wearing off.

'Ketty . . .' he said, his voice cracking as he spoke. 'Are you sure? Was Dylan sure?'

'Cal saw her . . . unconscious underwater,' I said, not looking up. 'How can you be unconscious underwater and survive?'

Nico shook his head.

After about twenty minutes, Jack returned.

'Where are the others?' Nico jumped up. 'What's happened to them?'

'Come with me, Ed,' Jack said, acting as if Nico hadn't spoken.

I stood up.

'Where are you taking him?' Nico's voice rose.

Jack still said nothing. I followed him out of the room. I didn't care where he took me. If Ketty wasn't in the world any more, what did it matter where I went?

Jack led me down a couple of corridors. I didn't take much notice of my surroundings, though I was aware that we were still in the warmer, furnished part of the castle. We went down a short flight of stairs to what I thought was the side of the building, and through a large fire door.

I found myself in another corridor. This one was painted plain white and had a clinical feel, completely different from the rooms through which we'd come. Jack arrived at a swing door. He pushed it open and ushered me inside.

I looked around, shocked. We were inside some sort of laboratory. Two rows of counter tops, complete with sinks and pipes snaking out from the walls, stood in front of us. There were shelves neatly stacked with files, a couple of computers and two large microscopes. A row of barrels marked 'oil' stood against the far wall.

The window was barred, just like the room where Nico and I had waited upstairs. I looked through the glass to the glistening expanse of water outside. I thought of Ketty again and my heart gave a sick lurch.

'No questions, Ed?' Jack said lightly.

I turned to face him. 'Where's Ketty?' I said. 'What happened to her?'

Jack looked away. He was no longer wearing his sunglasses – there was no need. My mind-reading abilities were redundant, thanks to the Medutox, but I could tell he felt uncomfortable. Was that because of Ketty?

'Why won't you tell me what happened to her?' I said.

The door behind me opened. I spun round. A tall, thick-set man with intense grey eyes walked into the room. He held out his hand to shake mine, smiling at the look of shock on my face.

'Hello, Ed,' he said. 'Remember me?'

14: The Duel

The man who had just walked into the lab was Damian Foster. I'd come up against him a few months ago, when the four of us in the Medusa Project had been investigating him and his company, Fostergames.

Foster was no ordinary criminal. He wasn't interested in money or power, just in doing whatever it took to get his brother out of prison. And he had the most powerful ability to block my mind-reading skills that I'd ever come across.

I realised my mouth had fallen open and closed it. Beside me, Jack Linden chuckled.

'This is the man I've been working for, Ed,' he said.

'*You?*' I stared at Foster, remembering the last time we'd met. It had been a battle to see inside his mind and then an even greater fight to break the connection as he – against all my other experiences of telepathy – managed to hold *my* mind with his.

'How are you, Ed?' Foster said.

I thought of Ketty.

'What's happened to the others – Cal and Dylan and . . . and Ketty?' I said, wondering if he would tell me the truth. If what Dylan had said was accurate, then the guards who swam after them must have found Ketty's body. In fact – and my stomach gave a sick lurch as I thought this – Ketty's body was probably in the castle, right now.

Foster raised his eyebrows. 'You've been in touch with Dylan and Cal?' he asked, though it sounded more like a statement than a question. 'You want to know what happened to Ketty?'

I looked him in the eye. Whatever he was going to say next, there was no way I could trust him. Part of me couldn't wait until my last Medutox spray wore off in a few minutes so that I could leap inside Foster's head and find out exactly what he knew. But part of me was scared. I didn't ever want to feel trapped and out of control, like I had during my previous telepathic session with him.

Foster sighed. 'I'm sorry to have to be the one to break the news, but as you obviously already know – Dylan and Cal have escaped, taking our recruit, Tania, with them. Ketty was not so lucky.' He paused. 'It's a shame. She was a lovely girl.'

Hurt and fury rose inside me. 'You hypocrite,' I spat. 'You don't care about Ketty. You don't care about any of us. You're just using us.'

'Is that what you think?' Foster sighed again. 'It's not quite that straightforward, Ed.'

103

'No?' I shouted. 'What was all that about with the train, then? Jack Linden said one of the reasons for crashing it was to demonstrate our powers to that Mr Ripley, so that he'd give you more money for your research. Which is obscene, because you've already made that boy unconscious.'

Foster shook his head. 'Bradley isn't unconscious any more,' he said. 'He's come through it now.' I followed his gaze. He was looking through to the next room. 'Bradley, come out here, please,' he called.

I watched, open-mouthed again, as a boy of about thirteen, with dark hair and pale skin, walked through the door. He looked tired – there were dark shadows under his grey eyes – and skinny, but his expression was bright and fierce.

'This is my brother's son, Bradley,' Foster said. 'You remember my brother, don't you, Ed? My brother, Rick?'

I nodded. Rick was the reason we'd come up against Foster before. Rick was in prison and Foster had been trying to blackmail the government – by setting off a bomb – into letting him go.

'Rick died in prison last month,' Foster said flatly. 'So I'm looking after his boy.'

He turned to Bradley. I followed his gaze. There was something hostile in Bradley's grey eyes, so like Foster's own I realised. But the boy was also scared.

You have to tell me how to see your thoughts.

I jumped. The Medutox had worn off and the boy was inside my head.

How are you doing that? I thought-spoke.

104

Bradley shrugged. I could sense his confusion through his presence in my mind.

The Medusix gave me the ability to speak without words, Bradley thought-spoke. *But I can't mind-read ... see into anyone's thoughts or feelings ... like my uncle says you can.*

I could barely believe it. So Medusix really worked. I remembered the reports we'd found online.

What about telekinesis? I thought-spoke, remembering the reports of the car moving, undriven, across the car park.

I can do that too. I moved a car and some tools the other day – and look ... Bradley broke the connection between us and turned towards one of the barrels of oil that stood against the far wall. He held out his hand and carefully raised the barrel up into the air. It wobbled about for a bit, then he slowly transported it a metre across the floor and set it down again. *I'm working on all my skills so I can help my uncle.*

Help him do what?

'Well done, Bradley,' Foster said with a warmth that surprised me. 'That's really coming on.' He looked at me. 'The oil is the base ingredient for the Medusix ... the delivery mechanism, if you like. We add various chemicals and our best approximation of the code for the Medusa gene and then the recipient takes a regular dose.' He waved his hand, indicating a row of thick glass bottles on a nearby shelf. 'Our stocks of Medusix. It takes a lot of effort to create enough even for one person. The oil helps us dilute the drug so it can go further, without losing its potency.'

I turned to Jack Linden. He had a huge grin on his face and was obviously enjoying how shocked I was. I looked back at Foster.

'You made the Medusix work, after all,' I said dully. My mind whirled with the possibilities this could give Foster ... the terrible, massive consequences of this power. In an instant I knew I had to see inside his mind, to find out – without giving him a chance to lie to me or prepare first – what exactly his plans were.

I made eye contact. Seconds later I was inside Foster's mind. I felt his surprise – then his whole brain seemed to withdraw. I can't explain it any other way, but it felt like he darted behind a wall where I couldn't reach him.

Well, he wasn't getting away from me that easily. I gritted my teeth and focused all my energy on getting past the 'wall'. Foster's resistance was strong. I was immediately catapulted back to the day, several months ago, when I had gone inside his mind before. Then I had felt him grip my own thoughts and feelings, able to control my own.

This time I was going to show him that *I* was in charge. I mentally slid across the wall he was creating, looking for cracks. In the lab I could hear voices. There was Bradley, asking his uncle what was going on. But Foster didn't reply. I wasn't letting him speak.

You've got stronger, Ed. Foster's thought-speech was admiring.

Whatever. I was in no mood for his flattery. I carried on

scanning his defences. There had to be a weakness . . . something he wasn't able to hide from me.

There. I saw my chance and I took it. I caught the tail of a thought about my own increased power and rode it past the wall, which seemed to dissolve as I saw deeper. Seconds later Foster's thoughts were laid bare.

And I saw his plan.

A moment after that and Foster was pushing me away again, constructing another wall. I wavered, distracted by the horror of what I'd seen. As my focus dwindled, Foster's resistance to me increased again. The wall went up. I felt suddenly, totally exhausted.

Ketty? I asked.

Dead, came the reply.

I broke the connection, sick to my stomach. I turned away, panting. Foster was also gasping for breath. Clearly the encounter had taken as much out of him as of me.

A tense silence fell on the lab. I was vaguely aware of Jack Linden and Bradley watching us intently, but I didn't look up. I'd seen Foster's plan and – under terrible pressure – he'd admitted Ketty was gone.

I couldn't remember ever feeling worse in my life.

'Your powers have increased exponentially since we last duelled,' Foster said. Again, that note of admiration in his voice. 'I'm impressed with what you can do. You'll make a great teacher for Bradley.'

I looked up. 'I'm not teaching Bradley *anything*,' I spat. 'I've seen what you're going to use him to do.'

Another tense silence. And then Foster smiled.

'Take Ed back to his room,' he said. 'Give him some time to think it over.'

'I don't need time,' I said. 'There's nothing you can do to me that'll make me cooperate.'

This wasn't strictly true, of course. I could just imagine how long I'd last if Foster started threatening Nico in front of me. Still, at that moment I was so angry I didn't care what I did or said. I just wanted to defy him.

Jack took me back to the room. Nico jumped up as I walked in. He looked better than before, though the bruise on his face was really coming out now – a mass of dark purple against his olive skin.

'Ed, are you all right?' he said, rushing over as Jack slammed the door shut on me. Needless to say, I'd been sprayed with Medutox on the way back.

'I'm fine,' I said. I paced up and down, past the brocade sofa. The enormity of Foster's plan was sinking in.

'Did Jack tell you about Ketty?' Nico asked. 'Is ... is it really true?'

'I think it is.' I stopped pacing and turned to face him.

Nico's eyes burned through me. I couldn't bear the pain in his expression.

'Tell me what Jack said.' His voice faltered as he spoke.

'It wasn't Jack who told me. It was Foster,' I said. 'He's the man behind all this ... the one Jack's working for.'

Nico looked dazed as I described how Foster and I had communicated telepathically. He nodded when I reported what I'd seen in Foster's mind about Ketty, but said nothing.

I didn't want to think about it any more, so I kept talking, explaining that Foster's nephew, Bradley, was no longer unconscious *and* was in possession of a range of basic psychic skills. 'I'm not sure what else he can do, but definitely a bit of telepathy and telekinesis,' I said. 'It was him who moved that car and those workman's tools – the telekinesis we heard about that brought us to Lovistov.'

'And Foster wants us to train him up further?' Nico spoke at last, his voice full of bitterness. '*That's* what he's brought us here for?'

'Not exactly.' I took a deep breath. It was hard to speak Foster's plan out loud. Somehow that made the insanity of it real. 'Foster wants us to train Bradley so he can lead an army of kids, all of whom will be given the Medusix. Foster's sending his men out right now to recruit more children – like Jack recruited Tania.'

Nico frowned. 'Why does Foster want an army of kids?' he asked.

'He wants to create a hit squad,' I explained. 'It's his revenge on the government and people like judges for letting his brother Rick die in prison.'

'You mean he's going to turn a bunch of random kids into psychic soldiers to . . . to kill people?' Nico said.

'Exactly,' I said. 'And we're part of the training team.'

Nico shook his head. His eyes lost their blank look and filled with a new fury. 'We can't let this happen, Ed. Apart from anything else, we can't let him trick innocent children into running away from their homes and then brainwash them into becoming murderers.' His voice shook. 'We have to stop him ... for Ketty's sake.'

I thought back to the lab, to the stocks of Medusix on the shelves and to the big tubs of oil standing in the corner.

'I know we have to stop him,' I said. 'And I've just worked out how.'

15: A Lesson

My plan was straightforward – if crazily ambitious. Somehow Nico and I had to get into the lab and destroy the stocks of Medusix before Foster conned more kids into joining his embryonic hit squad and then experimented on them.

'We can use the oil that's in there to cause an explosion. That'll get rid of the Medusix *and* all the equipment.'

'Foster and Jack are bound to have back-up stocks,' Nico said.

Since I'd come up with my plan he hadn't mentioned Ketty, but I could see the pain in his eyes and hear it in the reckless bitterness of his voice.

'I don't think they have stocks,' I said. 'And, before they can get everything they need to make the drug again, we'll be able to get the police involved.'

'What about Dylan and Cal?' Nico asked. 'And Amy back in Australia? Don't you think they'll already have gone to the police?' His voice cracked. 'Man, d'you think they'll have called Ketty's parents?'

'I guess so.' I took a deep breath, trying to keep my focus on the plan. 'But even if the police know where we are, it's still going to take time for them to reach us. And Foster's going to give Medusix to the new kids as soon as they're here.'

Nico looked up. Misery was etched into his face. 'Right,' he said, his eyes hardening again. 'So how do we get back to the lab?'

'Easy, we go outside to give Bradley his psychic skills lesson – then you teleport me up to the lab and I set the oil barrels on fire.'

Nico stared at me. 'How are you going to cause the explosion?'

I fished in my pocket for the lighter I'd stolen earlier. It was still there, tucked snugly beside the student's wallet. 'With this,' I said. 'And a bit of luck. You'll have to stay free from Medutox to teleport me out of the lab again afterwards.'

'But there are bars on the lab window,' Nico said. 'I can't get you past them.'

My heart sank. I hadn't considered that. 'Okay, then I'll have to make my own way up there while you cause a distraction. I'll find my own way out too.'

'What's happened to you, Ed, man?' Nico said with a wondering shake of the head. For a second, he looked like his old self again. 'You've gone all ... all action hero.'

'No I haven't,' I said, feeling my cheeks reddening. 'It's just we have to stop Foster and Jack. It'll be some kind of justice for Ketty.'

Nico's face fell. I bit my lip, wishing I hadn't mentioned her name.

'Okay,' he said. 'A distraction will work. All we need is our powers back.'

In the end it was hours before Jack reappeared, though a guard stepped inside the room at regular intervals to feed us and spray us with Medutox. There was no sign of Dylan and Cal – I had no idea what had happened to them and, without my Medusa powers, no way of finding out.

When Jack finally returned, we told him we were ready to give Bradley some lessons in telepathy and telekinesis. Jack looked cautiously pleased and – as the sun set over the lake – he brought Foster and Bradley to our room. They were accompanied by two guards I didn't recognise.

I glanced at the five of them, feeling suddenly anxious. It was going to be hard enough to get up to the lab without being seen – but completely impossible to get away from all these people without someone raising an alarm.

'This won't work,' Nico said. He sounded convincingly hard-headed. Over the past few hours I'd watched him bury his pain over Ketty too deep to surface easily. 'We can't stay inside. I need more space to do telekinesis.'

'And having all these people watching doesn't help either,' I added.

'The guards and I are staying,' Foster said firmly. 'But we can go outside where there's more room and Jack can go and check on plans for accessing our new kids.'

I glanced at Nico again. So they were already targeting a new batch of guinea pigs to experiment on. We had to move quickly. I turned to Bradley, determined to show a convincing level of interest in his abilities.

'So ... er, what does the Medusix taste like?' I asked him.

He blinked, clearly surprised I'd spoken directly to him. 'Like rotten vegetables,' he said with a grimace. 'It's disgusting. I have to take it every morning and every eve—'

'No need to explain everything,' Foster said, cutting him off. 'Let's get on.'

We went downstairs. As we walked past the doorway where I'd last seen Ketty, I felt a terrible pang. How could this place ... these people ... still be here, and not her?

I followed Nico and Foster outside, to the front of the castle. It was dark outside now and almost exactly thirty minutes since we'd both been sprayed with Medutox. I tried to reach Nico through remote telepathy. At first I thought it wasn't working, but as I focused, I soared into his mind – familiar to me now. As usual, it was intense and forceful. But now a darkness – the colour of his pain – touched everything like a shadow.

Shall I start? I suggested telepathically. *I could do some basics with Bradley. Hopefully Foster will relax if it's all going okay. Then you take over. Let me know when you're about to cause the distraction. Yes?*

Fine.

114

I broke the connection. 'Okay, Bradley,' I said. 'I'm going to mind-read you now; that should help you see how getting fully into someone's mind works, rather than just speaking without words, which you can already do.'

I glanced at Foster. He nodded his assent. I turned back to Bradley and met his gaze. With a *whoosh*, I was inside his head.

He sensed me straight away. I waited a moment, letting him get used to my presence. His mind was younger than he looked. Restless ... enquiring ... this boy was smart and unhappy. I probed a little further, letting the rush of his feelings wash over me. Like most people being mind-read for the first time, his thoughts were jumping about.

How is this working? What can you see? How much further can you go?

I can go wherever I want, I thought-spoke, probing a little deeper. Why was Bradley so unhappy? I caught the tail of his misery and rode it to a memory: saying goodbye to his father, Rick ... a blonde woman – I sensed she was his mother – in tears ... yes, there was pain inside Bradley. He missed his father. He wanted to be with his mother. He was scared of his uncle. Or was he just scared of being part of his uncle's plans?

You know what Foster wants to do is crazy, I thought-spoke. *And wrong.*

It's what I have to do, Bradley thought-spoke back. *I thought you were going to teach me how to mind-read.*

I hesitated. The last thing I wanted was to encourage

Foster's protégé to develop such a powerful skill. On the other hand, Bradley would be useful, if I could just get him on our side.

Okay, I thought-spoke. *I'm going to make my mind as open to you as I can. Just relax and try to catch a thought.*

I sat back in Bradley's mind, trying to keep my own thoughts under control. If I was honest, I was more than a little intrigued. How much would Bradley – whose abilities had been given to him via a drug rather than through genetic inheritance – be able to achieve?

It took a moment before I felt his presence, pushing gently into my mind. As soon as I sensed him, I resisted. No way did I want this boy seeing into any of my thoughts and feelings. I pushed him away – no problem, he was too weak to resist – and broke the connection.

Bradley gasped. He staggered backwards a little.

'You okay, Brad?' Foster's voice was full of concern.

'I'm fine,' Bradley said, a wide smile spreading over his face. 'That was amazing. Can we go again, Ed?'

I shook my head and glanced over at Foster. 'Not too much too soon. He needs a chance to get used to what he can do. Otherwise it'll be overwhelming.'

I was lying, of course. If I were Bradley I'd have wanted to practise going further . . . seeing how far I could penetrate into somebody's mind. But I wanted to hand over the lesson to Nico now . . . to find some way of fading into the background and getting away.

Foster looked at me shrewdly. I met his gaze, resisting the

116

slight pull to dive into his mind that always came whenever I made eye contact with anyone.

'Fine,' Foster said. 'Ed's right, Brad. You don't want to overdo it.' He turned to Nico. 'You're on.'

As Nico drew himself up, Foster signalled to one of the guards who stepped forwards and sprayed me with Medutox. *No.* My heart skipped a beat. Now I was going to have to cause the explosion without being able to contact Nico – or any of the other Medusa teens. I'd been hoping to have a moment to try Amy again – or Dylan. But now I'd have to wait.

Nico was looking right at Bradley. There was an intimidating intensity to his glare. 'Show me what you can do,' he demanded.

Bradley raised his hand. It was shaking slightly. He was obviously nervous performing in front of Nico. He pointed at a branch lying on the ground. It twitched, but didn't rise into the air as I'd seen the barrel of oil move earlier. It struck me that Medusix might confer a wider range of abilities than the Medusa gene, but not to the same level. I mean, okay, so Bradley hadn't had his powers for very long, but he didn't seem very effective in his control of them.

'I can't do it,' Bradley said.

Foster waved the guards back and moved closer to his nephew – a protective gesture. I smiled to myself. It was clever of Nico to make Bradley feel vulnerable, guessing correctly that this would draw Foster in.

Nico began explaining some of the basic principles of telekinesis.

117

'Let your mind be still,' he said. 'Relax your body. Focus, but don't grasp at it. Don't force what you're doing.'

I took a step away from them. One of the guards clocked me straight away. He held up his hand. Sunlight glinted off the gun in his palm. I gulped. Nico was going to have to make his distraction good to give me enough time to make it back into the castle.

I bit my lip, waiting. Nico was standing behind Bradley now, demonstrating a curving arm movement.

'This is the best, most economical move to help you with lifting stuff,' he said. 'Of course it's perfectly possible to do telekinesis without physically moving, but the hand gestures help.'

Bradley nodded, then focused on the stick on the ground again.

Nico glanced up. Caught my eye. Even without my telepathy I knew what was coming. I braced myself.

With a roar, Nico jumped back, away from Bradley. He raised both hands, twisting them at the wrists. Foster, just a few metres away, flew up into the air. Nico swung him round, teleporting him straight at the guard behind. With a smart crack, Foster's legs made contact with the guard's gun arm. The gun flew onto the grass. In an instant Nico tele-ported it up, driving it through the air and against the second guard who staggered backwards, his gun also falling to the ground. A moment later all three men and both guns were in the air, whirling over the grass. With a roar, Nico flung them all into the lake. He held out his hands, creating waves that

118

crashed across the water. The whole scene was chaos ... stones and branches flew up from the paving nearby ... It had only taken seconds.

Bradley ran to the side of the lake. 'Stop it!' he shouted.

Without looking round, Nico yelled out.

'Ed, go!'

I didn't need to be told twice. I turned and ran for the castle.

16: The Lab

I glanced round as I reached the main castle door. All hell was breaking out behind me. The men in the lake were yelling at the tops of their voices as Nico kept creating waves that crashed down on them. Beside him, Bradley was jumping up and down, emitting panicky shrieks. As I stood, watching, Broken Nose came racing round the corner. He didn't notice me. All his attention was on Nico and the furore at the lake. I sped indoors. Across the hall. Through the door. Up the stairs. Along the corridor.

I took a wrong turn and doubled back. Where was the door to the lab?

Around another corner and I saw it. I burst through the swing door and darted along the corridor. I reached the lab and skidded to a halt. I rattled the door handle. It was locked. For a terrible second I felt overwhelmed with a sense of failure. I needed Nico to open this lock. He *always* sorted out locks. Without him, I was useless.

Then I examined the door. It wasn't made of proper wood

and it didn't look particularly strong or well-made. Not like the internal doors in the older part of the castle. My dad's a builder and he's taught me a thing or two about construction. And this door was far from solidly put together. Confidence rising, I took a step back and aimed a kick at the weakest part of the door – just to the side of the keyhole.

With a splintering crack, the door flew open. Buoyed up by my success I rushed into the lab. Everything was just as it had been earlier. Moonlight from outside created long shadows across the oil barrels and the bottles of Medusix on the shelf. The night air was still filled with shouts and yells from outside. I raced over to the window. I could just make out Nico and Bradley, still on the shore of the lake. The bars were immovable, but at least I could push open the glass. As I did so, a cacophony of roars and yells floated up at me.

Nico was holding off the others, continuing to use his telekinesis to create chaos outside. I ran over to the shelf and switched on the light. It took a second to find all the Medusix bottles. *There.* I took the first two and raced to the sink in the corner of the room. Whatever else happened, I had to make sure all these stocks were destroyed. I flung both bottles into the sink. As their contents drained away, I raced back for two more. And another. There were five bottles in total and in less than ten seconds the contents of all of them were down the sink.

I scanned the empty shelf, then the surrounding area. No more Medusix. Just bottles of chemicals, each carefully labelled. There were acids and hormone extracts and all manner of liquids I'd never heard of. A small pot at the end of another shelf caught my eye: StopMed. I grabbed it. Was this more of the Medusix drug in a different container? I lifted the lid and peered in. A small sachet of pale pink powder met my eyes. It didn't look anything like Medusix but it carried a label of dosage instructions. For a second, I was tempted to chuck it down the sink as well. But the sachet was tiny. And I was curious. What else was Foster developing here? I took the sachet out of the pot and shoved it in my pocket.

The yells outside in the lake were loud and angry. Nico was still, clearly, holding off all the guards. All I had to do now was set light to the oil in the barrels and hope the fire took hold as fast as possible. I grabbed the nearest barrel and braced myself, ready to tip it over. To my horror, it lifted in my hands – as light as a shoebox. I tore off the lid. *No.* The oil barrel was empty. I raced to the next and the next. Also empty.

I looked round desperately. What could I use to start a fire now? There was nothing. I could attempt to light one of the cloths on the counter or the white coat hanging on the back of the door, but a single glance at the ceiling confirmed a sprinkler system was in place. Without something to create a proper blaze, a fire would be extinguished before it had a chance to take hold.

I stopped for a second. I had to think bigger. There were other rooms. Other sources of fuel. I dashed back into the

122

corridor, then out, into the properly furnished part of the castle. I could hear some of the guards yelling downstairs. I strained my ears, but I couldn't make out any sounds from the lake.

Was Nico still out there? Was he okay? And where were Dylan and Cal? Hours had passed since they'd escaped. Had they managed to reach the police? Was help on its way?

If only I had my Medusa ability back I'd be able to check in with all of them. But there was no time to think about the others. I *had* to find a way of destroying the lab. One of the guards pounded up the stairs. I ducked back, behind a wall, holding my breath as he raced past. He skidded to a halt just metres away from me. He pulled a key from his key chain and slid it into a door. I watched intently as he dashed into the room. Seconds later he was out again, a rifle clutched in his hand, running full pelt back down the corridor. He hadn't noticed me at all.

As the guard disappeared down the stairs, I crept over to the room he'd gone into. He'd left it unlocked, the door ajar. I pushed it open. *Wow.* It was some sort of arsenal. I looked around, stunned. There was a rack of guns, still chained into position, and a cupboard containing knives and chains. Without stopping to think, I ran to the cupboard and smashed the glass. I yanked open the door and peered inside. What could I use? My eyes lit on a hand grenade on the bottom shelf. It was small and oval, with a pin sticking out of the top. I'd never used a hand grenade before but I'd seen them in action movies a million times and I knew how they worked. You pulled out the pin and threw the grenade. Seconds later it exploded – a tiny bomb. It was perfect for destroying the lab.

I ran to the door, clutching the hand grenade. The castle was eerily still. No sounds came from outside. Did that mean Nico had taken his chance to escape? Or that he'd been recaptured?

As I turned, ready to head for the lab, Knife Man appeared, blocking my way. I darted back, my breath catching in my throat. Had he seen me?

I peered around the wall. No, he hadn't noticed me, but he was now stationed outside the lab. It was going to be impossible for me to get past him and carry out my original plan. I hesitated. What on earth could I do now?

I thought fast. Maybe if I could run outside and hurl the grenade up at the lab window ... The light was on in the room, so it should be easy to identify, and even I should be able to hit such a big target.

It wasn't a perfect plan, but it was the best I had.

I raced along the corridor and back down the stairs to the ground floor of the castle. I darted out through the front door. There was no sign of anyone.

I took a backwards step, looking up to the first floor. The lab was easy to spot. It was the only room in the row with the light on and the window open. I steadied my hand, ready to hurl the grenade. Out of the corner of my eye I could see Broken Nose rushing towards me round the side of the castle. A yell from behind. I spun round. Another guard. Almost on top of me. I had no time. I pulled the pin out of

124

the grenade. Drew back my arm. But before I could release the grenade the guard behind me reached me. Grabbed me round the waist. Twisted me round.

Completely disoriented, I flung the grenade away from me. It soared through the air as I was hurled to the ground. I looked up, dust flying into my eyes. The grenade seemed to be moving in slow motion, heading towards the far corner of the building. Miles away from the lab.

Boom! Seconds later the grenade hit the castle wall about six metres up. The explosion boomed through the air. Brick and stone flew everywhere, fire rocketing out of the wall. At the same time, appearing from nowhere around the side of the castle, Dylan ran into view.

I opened my mouth to yell, but the world was exploding in front of my eyes, drowning me out – and burying Dylan under tons of stone.

DYLAN

17: Buried

I ran along the castle wall, hidden from view. I had to get to Ed. I checked my force field was fully engaged.

Boom! As I raced round the corner, a huge explosion threw me off my feet. Rubble fell on my head. Down and down. I crouched low, hands instinctively over my head, praying that my force field would protect me.

It did. I had no idea what had happened, but it felt like the castle wall I was running past had fallen on top of me. It was still coming down. I could hear the final few thuds of stone on stone, but I couldn't see a thing.

I was buried alive.

The energy flowing from deep inside me, covering my whole body, was all that was keeping me from being totally crushed. As I thought this, I nearly panicked and lost my focus. Dust and powder from the stones seeped through my force field. I could feel the fine silt settling on my hair ... my skin. I took a few slow breaths, trying to calm down. Okay, so inside the mound of earth and stone it was pitch black and there was a ton of rubble above me but I was still alive.

Stay calm and think, I told myself. I steadied my energies and tried to work out what to do. Maybe Ed would attempt to make contact with me. Except ... if he'd been overpowered by the guards he would probably have been sprayed with Medutox.

As my fears whirled round my head I could feel my force field weakening. More rubble dust settled on me, on my face, in my throat, choking me. *Stop it*, I ordered myself. *There has to be a way out of this. Think.*

It had been Nico's telekinetic 'lake storm' that had attracted my attention, but it was Ed – and the guard attacking him – who I'd been running towards.

Had any of them actually seen me coming round the corner before the building above my head exploded? Did they even know I was buried under here?

Cal certainly didn't. He'd flown off with Tania earlier, to take her to the local police so she could get back to her family. I'd waited across the lake all day, expecting him to return – hopefully with police support – but he hadn't shown up.

Panic rose inside me again. The air around me was thick and hot. My force field protects me from the larger stuff, but it doesn't work on a molecular level. That's why Medutox affects me – I can't help but breathe it in. Basically, even with my force field I still need oxygen. And there wasn't any in here.

I pushed cautiously at the stones above my hand. There was no way I could move them. They were just too heavy. A terrible sense of claustrophobia swamped me, tightening my chest and throat. *It's okay*, I tried to reassure myself. Maybe I couldn't claw my way out of this. But I had my force field. That was a start.

'Dylan! Dylan!' Ed's yell was muffled. 'Are you okay?'

'Yeah, I'm great, Chino Boy,' I shouted, relief flooding through me. 'Is Nico with you?' I was trying to sound calmer than I actually felt. I wondered if Ed could tell. He's kinda perceptive, I've realised recently.

'No,' Ed yelled back. 'But don't worry.'

My heart sank. Ed might be perceptive, but he's not exactly the physical type. If it was down to him to dig me out of here it might take hours.

'Are you alone?' I asked.

'Er . . . no,' Ed said. 'The guards and Jack are here.'

From bad to worse. My one hope was that Ed might have overpowered his guard and that he and Nico were free. Now I was going to be just as much a prisoner as they were.

A tiny chink of light appeared overhead as a large stone shifted. I could hear footsteps. And then the dark sky opened up above my head. A bright light shone down.

'Dylan?' It was Jack Linden himself: Harry's dad and a total pig of a man, as far as I was concerned.

'Get that flashlight out of my eyes!' I snapped.

'I take it you're all right?' Jack said drily.

'Peachy, thanks,' I said, trying to sound braver than I felt.

131

A huge piece of masonry right in front of me was dragged away from the pile. I heard it thud onto the ground as rubble fell around me, filling the gap the stone left.

'Be careful,' I yelled.

'Aren't you using your force field?' Jack asked.

I grimaced. Jack had always known and understood far too much about our Medusa abilities. I'd liked him so much when I'd first met him – he was interesting and exciting and was offering me a totally new life. Plus he was my godfather – once a good friend of my parents. To be honest, though I'd never admitted it to anyone, I was hurt that he'd betrayed us. Upset that he had put his own self-interest before his loyalty to my mom and dad.

'Is she okay?' That was Ed. It sounded like he was just a few metres away from the rubble.

'I'm great,' I shouted. 'Though I think I may have broken a nail or two.'

Above my head, Jack laughed. Another huge shift in the masonry around me. Now I could see the sky above clearly: half a moon and some stars across a ragged circle of navy. Ten seconds later and there was a big enough gap to pull me through. Hands reached in and clutched at my arm. I released the force field around my wrist and let myself be hauled up and out of the rubble. I scrambled the last bit, onto the pile of stones, then half climbed, half slid back down to the ground. I was free.

The men who had dug me out were staring open-mouthed. I could see why as I looked back at the heap that had smothered me. Surrounded by other debris, it was at least two metres high. I shivered, realising that without my Medusa ability I would undoubtedly have been killed under all those stones.

Jack was standing a few metres away, silhouetted against the light from the castle.

'Welcome back, Dylan,' he said with that smooth smile I knew so well.

I ignored him, turning instead to Ed who stood nearby, his arm held by Broken Nose.

'Where's Nico?' I said.

'Inside, I think,' Ed said. 'We both got sprayed again,' he added.

I gave him a curt nod. My mind had gone back to the last communication we'd had – about Ketty. I didn't want to think about her . . . about Cal's face as he'd come out of the lake that last time.

Cal. Where on earth *was* he? He was supposed to be bringing the local police so we could rescue Ed and Nico. I glanced out over the lake, wondering if he was on his way at last. Jack followed my gaze.

'Time to go,' he said. 'We're leaving the castle. Now.'

'Where are we going?' Ed asked.

'Hey!' I spun around. 'Not so fast. I need a shower. Not to mention some fresh nail polish.'

It was vital we didn't leave until Cal and the police arrived. For the first time since I set off for the castle I regretted running over here. If I'd kept my distance and watched the commotion rather than getting caught up in it, I would have been able to spy on Jack as he left with Nico and Ed – discovering useful things such as the licence number of his car and his direction of travel.

'No shower,' Jack said shortly.

'But look at me,' I said. 'I'm a total mess.' It was true though not, of course, my main reason for wanting the delay. My hair and clothes were covered in dust from the rubble I'd just been under and there was a layer of grey silt on my face.

'No shower,' Jack repeated. And then he stepped forward and sprayed me with Medutox. I engaged my force field but – as before – it was impossible to prevent the fine Medutox mist from entering my airway.

One of the guards gripped my arms. Before I knew what was happening, a car swerved round the corner. It backed up in front of us and Ed and I had sacks shoved over our heads. We were bundled inside. From the voices outside I could tell Nico was being forced into the seat behind. At least the three of us were together.

But as the car drove off, it struck me that now there was no way for Cal or anyone else to find us.

We were worse off than ever.

18: An Old Friend

The car journey took just over an hour, but we stopped frequently along the way so I was guessing we had just travelled back to Lovistov. Ed and I didn't speak much, for fear of being overheard by whoever was driving. In the end I was so tired I fell into an uneasy sleep, waking every few minutes with a jolt of anxiety.

The sun was just rising when the car stopped for the last time and rough hands hauled me out of the back of the car. I could hear footsteps beside me. Ed was complaining about being pushed . . . Nico was protesting too. We were dragged up what felt like ten sets of stairs and shoved past a door. More rough hands removed the bindings round my wrists – and, at last, the blindfold.

I looked around as the guards who'd brought us here left the room. We were in a modern apartment. Sparsely but cleanly furnished with two sofas and a TV. A small kitchen area stood at one end of the room. A loaf of bread, a pint of milk and some plates containing slices of ham and cheese had been left out on the counter. I walked over to the window. There were no bars, at least, but the glass was thick – doubleglazed I was guessing – and the window itself locked. Outside was a narrow alley. The wall opposite – about two metres away – contained no windows as far as I could see. In fact, the only things I *could* see, apart from the concrete ground below, were a couple of black bins and the car we'd come in.

I turned around. Ed was examining the food on the kitchen counter. Nico was on his knees, peering at an air vent in the wall close to the floor.

'They're pumping Medutox through this,' he said. 'I can just feel the spray in the air coming through the air con.'

Ed held up the loaf of bread. 'D'you think this is okay to eat?' he said anxiously.

'It's eat or starve, Chino Boy,' I said. 'All I've had all day is a few carrots I found in this barn across the lake where Cal left me. Anyway, if they wanted to kill us, we'd already be dead. Now will you please tell me what the hell's been going on?'

As we devoured the food, Ed explained what had happened since we'd got separated. I wasn't all that shocked that Foster was attempting to set up some lunatic hit squad. I mean, the man had clearly been totally unhinged even before his brother died, when he was trying to blackmail the government to release him.

I explained that Cal had gone for help earlier and that I had no idea what had happened to him. 'He was supposed to make a phone call to Avery and Fergus in Australia and get the local police to go to the castle and rescue you guys.'

'At least he wasn't recaptured,' Ed said glumly.

There was a pause and then came the question I'd been dreading.

'So what happened with Ketty?' Nico said, not looking at me directly.

I took a deep breath. I didn't like remembering it. Let alone talking about it. Some things stick in your mind forever. And I already knew that, for me, one of those things would be Cal's face as he came out of the lake after failing to save Ketty.

'I already told Ed remotely,' I said, not wanting to go over it again.

Nico looked up at me. His expression was hard, but I could see the pain buried deep in his eyes.

'Okay.' I sighed. 'We had to swim under this fence in the water to get away from the castle. Ketty didn't surface, so Cal swam back for her. She was unconscious. Trapped under the fence. You'd have needed bolt cutters to get her free, which of course Cal didn't have. In the end he had to come up for air . . .' I paused. Both Nico and Ed were hanging on my words. I looked away. 'It was too late for Ketty. Cal had no choice.'

A terrible silence fell in the room. I don't think any of us knew what to say. I sure didn't. I hadn't let myself feel just how horrible it was to know Ketty was gone. I *couldn't* let myself. It wasn't like me and her were great friends. But we'd been through so much together. The original Medusa Project was her and me and Ed and Nico. Ketty not being with us left a huge hole – one I couldn't ever see being filled. Plus Ketty is ... was ... kind of cool.

Actually, she was one of the coolest people I'd ever met.

Ed cleared his throat. 'Er ... did either of you notice if Foster came into the house with us?'

'Nah.' Nico turned away. He moved over to the window and peered out at the little alley. I couldn't be sure, but I thought there were tears in his eyes. 'I definitely didn't hear Foster. Just Jack and the guards.'

'So what, Ed?' I knew I sounded way too aggressive. I mean, it was obvious Ed was just trying to change the subject away from Ketty. But sometimes, even when I don't want to sound angry, that's the sort of thing that comes out of my mouth.

Normally Nico would have snapped at me to shut up. But right then he said nothing. Just carried on staring out of the window. Ed was also looking away from me, gazing down at his plate of bread and cheese.

I wanted to say something to make everything okay. But even as I had that thought, I was also thinking that it didn't matter what I said or did, nothing was going to bring Ketty back.

And then the key turned in the lock and the door slowly opened.

Instinctively I tried to engage my force field in readiness

for whoever was about to come in, but of course – thanks to the Medutox – my ability wasn't working.

Nico turned around. Ed stood up.

And Harry Linden walked into the room.

The shock literally took my breath away. He looked straight at me.

'Hi,' he whispered.

I couldn't speak. I just stared at him. Harry and I are kind of going out. I say 'kind of' because we haven't got to spend very much time together so far, though we talked quite a lot in the last two weeks when I was in Australia and he was still at home in England. I wouldn't admit it to his face, but Harry's gorgeous. He's got these piercing blue eyes and the way he looks at me makes me melt.

'What are you doing here?' Nico said, looking as shocked as I felt.

'I've come to get you out,' Harry said, glancing at the door. He put his finger to his lips indicating we had to keep quiet. 'Come on, they're in the room next door.'

He led the way into the tiny hall. Voices came from the room to our left. My heart was in my mouth as I followed Harry, with Nico and Ed right behind. We tiptoed to the front door of the apartment. Harry punched a number into the keypad on the wall, then opened the door. We crept outside. Harry raced across the concrete hallway and pressed the button for the lift. A red light above the door showed it was rising from the sixth floor. The sign beside said we were on the tenth floor.

'Come on,' I muttered.

Nico looked warily around him.

'Shouldn't we take the stairs rather than wait?' Ed suggested.

Harry shook his head. 'One of the guards is out there having a smoke. He's supposed to stand by the front door, keeping watch, but he's always slipping off for a fag.' I followed his glance to the light above the lift. It had reached the eighth floor. I looked down and Harry met my gaze.

'Hey, Red,' he said with a smile.

'How did you find us?' I whispered, soaking up that smile. My heart was thudding – and not only because we were still standing outside the flat.

'I followed Dad,' Harry said softly.

I nodded. Harry's dad was, of course, Jack Linden. Once upon a time Harry's parents and mine had been good friends.

'Dad was really angry when I turned up here,' Harry went on, 'but he's let me stay until he's got time to get me on a flight home. I couldn't believe it when I heard them bring you guys in.'

The lift pinged to a stop in front of us. I glanced over my shoulder. No one appeared to have noticed we were missing. I felt Harry reach for my hand. I gave it a squeeze, my heart leaping. We were almost out. We were going to make it.

And then the lift door opened and I gasped in horror.

Foster was inside, his gun in his hand.

19: A New Hit

For a moment everyone froze. I don't know who was more shocked – Foster or us. Foster recovered quickly. He raised his gun.

'Get back,' he snarled, striding out of the elevator.

Again, I instinctively tried to engage my force field but nothing happened. I stood where I was. Harry grabbed my hand. For a second, all I was aware of was the feel of his fingers against mine. Luckily Nico was thinking smarter. He shoved Ed sideways. Ed stumbled. Foster's eyes shot to him. Nico darted forward and grabbed Foster's arm, knocking the gun to the ground.

'Run!' he yelled.

Harry and I turned together. We raced to the door leading to the stairs. But – as we reached it – the guard who'd been smoking out on the steps walked through. He barked something in his own language, clearly an order for us to stop. He lunged at Harry, shoving him backwards.

'Leave him alone!' I shouted.

'Enough.' Foster's voice stopped me in my tracks.

I turned round to face him. He was standing in the middle of the landing, his gun pointed at Nico's head. Ed stood helplessly to one side.

I held up my hands, my stomach in knots. Another attempt to escape Foster had ended in disaster.

For the first time since we'd arrived in Lovistov I wondered if we were ever going to get away from him. Or if the rest of us were going to die here, like Ketty. I pushed these dark thoughts away and held my head high. No way was I going to show Foster how vulnerable I really felt.

As the guard ushered us back inside and into the room we'd been locked into before, Harry's arm crept round my shoulder.

'You okay, Red?' he said.

'Sure,' I said. 'Why wouldn't I be? I've been a prisoner before.'

Harry shook his head. 'Don't give me that,' he said. 'I know about Ketty.'

I looked at him. I didn't know what to say. I felt like he could see right inside me – all the misery over Ketty and how Foster had trapped me – twice.

'I'm sorry I didn't get you out,' Harry said quietly.

I glanced around. Ed and Nico were sitting side by side on the couch, talking in low voices. Nico's head was in his hands. Neither of them were looking at us.

I looked back at Harry. 'I'm glad you're here,' I said.

Harry opened his mouth as if to say something, but before

he could, a shouting match started next door. Foster and Jack were yelling at each other. It was hard to work out what they were saying at first, as they were both speaking at once.

'He's my son,' Jack shouted. 'You can't lock him up.'

'He can't be trusted,' Foster yelled back. 'You're lucky I didn't kill him.'

I raised my eyebrows.

'That's you they're talking about, Harry,' Nico said from across the room.

Harry shrugged. 'Yeah,' he said, ultra-casually. But I could hear the fear behind the bravado.

After a few minutes, the yelling subsided. I half expected Jack to come storming through the door and drag Harry away. But of course Foster was never going to let him do that.

Harry himself grew very quiet as time passed. We talked for a bit about how he'd discovered Jack had hacked into his phone to find out whether we'd taken the bait to travel to Lovistov. Jack had already set off by then, but Harry did some hacking of his own – Jack had taught him a lot about how to do that several years ago, when they had a much better father-son relationship – and found out where Jack was staying. Harry traced him to this apartment where, until Foster's arrival just now, Jack had managed to keep him hidden.

'So Jack says Foster spends all his time at the castle?' Nico asked.

Harry nodded. 'Dad says he's obsessed with developing

the Medusix – that he's convinced he can use it to build this huge army of kids with psychic powers.'

'Why give the drug to children?' Ed asked.

'Because Medusix only works on kids,' Harry explained. 'It just makes adults unconscious for a few minutes.'

I nodded, remembering what Jack had told us earlier.

'Maybe also because he reckons he can boss kids around more,' Nico added with a snarl.

I caught his eye. 'Well, he's wrong about that, isn't he?'

The door opened. Foster and a skinny boy a bit younger than us stood in the doorway. I recognised the boy immediately from Ed's description of Foster's nephew and tensed, on guard in case he tried any telekinesis on me.

'Hi, Bradley,' Ed said.

Bradley scowled.

'You two,' Foster ordered, pointing at me and Harry. 'Out here.'

I glanced around at Ed and Nico. I could see both of them were prepared to put up a fight but Foster still had his gun and his guards stood behind him.

There was no point in resisting right now.

Harry took my hand. Foster led us into the room next door. It might once have been a bedroom but now there was no sign of a bed or indeed any furniture apart from a small white wardrobe that stood in the corner.

Harry and I stood together opposite Foster and Bradley. They didn't look much like each other. Foster oozed fury and arrogance. Bradley's eyes – though a similar grey to his uncle's – were shrouded in self-consciousness. He hadn't looked at me properly yet.

'Bradley's telekinesis skills are developing well, though he's still struggling with telepathic communication,' Foster said.

Despite everything I had to bite back a giggle. Foster sounded like a teacher giving a report on a child – with me and Harry as the parents.

'That means so much to me,' I said drily.

Foster pursed his lips. 'I want you to show him how to create a protective force field around himself, Dylan,' he said.

'I can't,' I said honestly. 'It didn't ... doesn't happen like that.'

Foster narrowed his eyes. 'I've spoken with Jack Linden. He *told* me he gave you guidance when he met you.'

'Sure,' I said. 'He got me to relax and focus on my breathing but that just helped bring what was already there to the surface. I mean, Bradley's welcome to try doing the same thing, but I don't see how it will work unless he's already got the ability.'

Foster looked at Bradley expectantly. Bradley chewed nervously on his lip. He closed his eyes and slowed his breathing.

A few seconds passed. Then he opened his eyes and shook his head. 'What does it feel like?'

'Like ... like an energy coming from inside you, going out all around you,' I said.

'What about extending the protection to others?' Foster snapped. 'I know you learned to do that after the original ability developed.'

'That's true,' I admitted. 'But I couldn't extend the force field until it existed in the first place.'

Bradley closed his eyes. Another few moments passed. He shook his head.

'I don't have that skill at all,' he said, looking embarrassed.

Foster tutted. 'Then Dylan will have to go on the job with you,' he said.

I exchanged an alarmed glance with Harry.

'What job?' I said.

'What are you going to make her do?' Harry spoke at the same time.

Foster threw him a nasty smile. 'Don't worry, Harry, you'll be with her. I'm sending you, Dylan and Bradley on the first hit squad mission.'

Foster explained his plan. We were to travel by helicopter to a nearby city where one of the politicians who had blocked the release of Foster's brother, Rick, from prison was attending an international conference.

'I want you to get past the doors and guards, let yourself into the cloakroom where they leave coats and bags and laptops . . . and hack into his computer,' Foster said. 'Bradley will deal with the lock, but the security is down to you, Dylan. You'll have to shield yourself and the others from the

146

infra-red laser system that the conference building uses to secure its private meeting rooms.'

'And I suppose you want me to hack into this politician's laptop and steal information off his computer?' Harry said angrily.

'Not at all,' Foster said. 'I want you to *plant* information. False information that will make everyone think the man has taken bribes to reveal state secrets.'

I opened my mouth but before I could speak, Foster had anticipated what I was going to say.

'Ed and Nico stay here,' he said. 'So long as you do what you're told, nothing will happen to them.'

And that was that.

We took off a couple of hours later. We were blindfolded for most of the journey – and it was impossible to talk properly over the sound of the helicopter engine, so I spent most of the ride wondering if there would be any chance to contact Fergus or Avery once we arrived ... after all, a private room in a conference building would surely have a phone ...

We were bundled into a car straight after landing. About fifteen minutes later our car stopped and our blindfolds were removed. We were in a side road. There was some passing traffic, but it wasn't busy. Foster was no longer with us, but Knife Man and another guard I hadn't seen before were. Knife Man indicated the fire door to the building on our left.

'In through there,' he said. 'Then you know what to do.'

Harry nodded. He looked nervous. As for Bradley, he was

shaking. I suddenly realised that of the three of us I was the only one with any kind of mission experience.

'We'll be fine,' I snapped.

We stood outside the door. I'm used to Nico unlocking stuff real fast now, but Bradley was taking ages. Harry drew me to one side. He glanced over at the men in the car. They were watching us intently, clearly under orders to make sure we got inside.

Harry stood real close to me. 'I was just thinking we should give Bradley a little space,' he said softly.

I gazed into his eyes. They're a bright blue – like I said – and they really sparkle, which sounds like a crazy cliché but happens to be true.

'I see you got a piercing since I saw you,' Harry said, staring at the stud in my nose.

My hand flew up to my face. Personally I think the tiny stud is gorgeous. I've had a few compliments on it – and a bit of teasing from Nico and Cal. Up until that moment I didn't care what anyone thought. Suddenly I very much wanted Harry to like it.

He raised his eyebrows. 'It looks cool,' he said.

'Like I'm bothered what you think,' I said. But I couldn't help myself smiling.

And I could tell Harry knew I was pleased because he smiled too.

I glanced over at Bradley. He was still trying to open the fire door.

'Any time this century, kiddo,' I muttered.

With a pop, the door opened. Bradley looked around at us triumphantly. 'We're in,' he said.

'Here goes.' Harry blew out his breath.

Suddenly I felt nervous too. Bradley's telekinesis was not going to work under any kind of real pressure, I could see. And though Harry was an IT genius as far as I was concerned, he didn't have any kind of special powers himself.

Which meant the mission – and the fate of Nico and Ed back in Lovistov – was basically down to me.

20: Mission Impossible

The inside of the building was cool and dark and empty. We were standing at one end of a corridor. I glanced at Bradley. He was trying to look composed but his hands were still trembling.

I shook my head. This was a freakin' babysitting mission.

Harry pointed towards the stairs at the other end of the corridor. 'Up there,' he whispered.

'I know,' I said. 'Stay behind me.'

We crept along the corridor. I kept my arms extended and my force field engaged, protecting all three of us as we walked. We came to a red laser security beam.

'Slowly, no sudden moves,' I ordered.

Harry and Bradley edged after me as I led them through the beam. My force field prevented the beam from sensing our presence. No problem. We reached the stairs. Voices and footsteps sounded from high above our heads. Bradley froze.

'Shouldn't we go back?' he whispered. 'Those people will see us.'

'We're only going up one storey, remember?' I hissed. 'Those voices are coming from further up the building.'

'Okay,' Bradley muttered.

I glanced at Harry. He gave me a swift, determined nod. If he was scared, he wasn't showing it.

'Let's go.' Harry grinned. 'This is cool.'

I shook my head. Harry being overexcited was potentially as dangerous as Bradley being ultra-anxious.

Up the stairs to the first-floor landing and through the second door on the left. So far so good. We hadn't seen anyone and clearly no one suspected we were here.

We were in another empty corridor. The door to the private set of rooms where we were headed was just a couple of metres away. It was marked Leindorf Suite. I took a deep breath. This was where Foster had directed us.

'I don't feel very well,' Bradley said.

I rolled my eyes. 'Just stay close,' I whispered.

'Take a few deep breaths,' Harry advised.

I reached the door to the Leindorf Suite and tried the handle. It was locked.

I stood back and gestured to Bradley. 'Open it,' I said. 'Fast.'

Bradley hesitated, then focused on the door. I watched him carefully. His forehead was pale and clammy-looking. It struck me that maybe the problem wasn't nerves after all. Maybe he genuinely wasn't well.

Bradley twisted his hand to the side in a gesture that reminded me of those I'd seen Nico make so often. To my surprise the door clicked open at the first attempt. Bradley turned to face me and Harry, a huge smile on his face.

'Good job,' I whispered. 'Now stay behind me.'

I pushed the door open very slowly and peered round it, into the empty room beyond. A table laden with cups and saucers and pots of coffee stood beside the wall. No sign of a phone. The room bent round at right angles. A man in a dark uniform was just visible walking into the other part of the room. His black shoes squeaked as he paced out of sight.

'There's a security guard,' I whispered, turning to Bradley. 'You'll have to distract him while Harry and I go past.'

'What?' Bradley's eyes filled with horror. 'Wait, I'm not read—'

But I was already through the door. I crept over to where the room angled round. The security guard was halfway to the door at the far end. There were two doors leading off on either side. It all looked exactly as Foster had outlined.

I glanced over my shoulder. Harry and a very alarmed Bradley were right behind me. As we stood, waiting, the guard's footsteps stopped. His shoes squeaked as he turned and then his slow pacing steps headed back towards us. He would come into view any second. A line of sweat trickled down my back.

I nudged Bradley. 'Ready?' I mouthed.

He shook his head. 'I'm not—'

'Go!' I pushed him out in front of me.

The security guard's footsteps stopped again. 'Who are you?' he barked. 'How did you get in here?'

I held my breath. Bradley said nothing. I peered round the corner. Bradley was staring into the guard's eyes, 'holding' his mind telepathically. The guard was staring back, a look of shock on his face. Knowing how uncertain Bradley had seemed, I was guessing we didn't have all that much time.

'Come on.' I tugged at Harry's arm.

We raced up to the guard. I drew his hands behind his back and tied them and his ankles with the handcuffs Foster had given me. Harry wound some tape across the guard's mouth. Sorted.

'Okay, Bradley, you can release him,' I said.

Bradley turned to me, his eyes glittering with feverish excitement. The guard tried to yell out, but he couldn't make a sound, thanks to his gag.

'That was amazing,' Bradley said. 'I didn't know I could do that.'

'I'm real happy for you,' I drawled, 'but right now we need to find a laptop.'

I quickly checked the first room on the left-hand side. As expected, it was a cloakroom containing a rail of coats and a few suitcases on the floor. I checked the picture of the laptop bag we were looking for, while Harry and Bradley bundled the guard inside the room. Harry took a third pair of handcuffs and chained him to the rail while I ran my eyes over the bags on the floor.

'It's not here,' I said. 'Let's go next door.'

We left the guard tied up and moved to the next room. It was some kind of meeting room – slightly larger than the cloakroom, with a central table around which about ten chairs had been arranged. No phones again, I noticed. A row of small bags stood against the far wall.

'We're looking for a dark green computer case with a star emblem on the side,' I reminded the others.

Bradley nodded. 'I'm going to have to sit down,' he said.

I stared at him. His face looked really sweaty now . . . and he was as white as the walls of the meeting room.

'Are you okay?' Harry asked.

'Sure,' Bradley said, but he didn't sound very convincing.

'You were awesome,' I said, thinking maybe I'd sounded a bit harsh earlier.

See . . . who says I can't be generous and encouraging?

'Thanks,' Bradley muttered. He sank to the floor and leaned against the wall.

'There it is.' Harry pointed to a dark green laptop bag at the end of the line of cases.

I followed his gaze. Sure enough, the side of the bag contained the star emblem Foster had told us about.

'Dylan, you better check no one's coming, yeah?' Harry said.

'Okay.' I rushed outside and peered up and down. According to Foster's information, the politician on whose laptop we were supposed to plant information would be through the door to my far left – in some high-level meeting. Foster had reckoned we would have about fifteen minutes to

154

get in and out of the building before anyone noticed us. We'd already used up five of those minutes.

As I raced back inside, Harry was taking the laptop out of the bag.

'No one in sight,' I said.

Harry laid the computer carefully on the table. He looked up at me and raised an eyebrow. 'So did you miss me, Red?'

'Get on with it,' I said.

Harry grinned and opened up the laptop. He switched it on and peered at the screen.

'Any time this century,' I said.

Harry threw me a sideways glance. 'Skip it, Red.'

I opened my mouth to retort, then thought better of it. Its not that I wanted to do what Harry told me. I was just aware of the hurry we were in.

Harry bent closer to the screen. He was muttering something under his breath, then he reached forward and tapped at the laptop keys.

'*Yes*!' he said softly.

'You found the right file already?' I said, genuinely impressed.

Harry nodded. He took the memory stick Foster had given him from his pocket and inserted it into the side of the laptop. He looked up at me. 'Just two more minutes,' he said.

I checked my watch. We only had six minutes until the time Foster had predicted the meeting would break up. Bradley was still slumped against the wall by the door, his eyes glazed over and his face unnaturally pale. He looked almost out of it. Maybe giving him something to do would help.

'Would you check on that guard in the cloakroom?' I asked him.

Bradley nodded and struggled to his feet. He didn't seem that steady as he disappeared out of the room.

Harry gave a low whistle. 'Done,' he said. 'I added all the info we were given to the file. Anyone reading it will think the man who wrote it has committed fraud on a massive scale.'

'Fast work,' I said.

Harry looked at me as he removed the memory stick and placed the laptop back in its bag. 'I'm good at this, Red,' he said. '*Really* good.'

I could feel my cheeks flushing. 'Let's go,' I said.

Harry put the laptop bag back where we found it and we raced out of the room.

Bradley was just emerging from the cloakroom next door. If anything, he looked even worse than before. I was about to ask if he was all right, when the door at the end of the room opened. A man in a suit strode in. He saw us straight away, his mouth falling open in shock.

I grabbed Harry and Bradley. 'Run!' I shouted.

As we raced to the door I extended my force field, making sure all three of us were protected. I didn't look round. Back into the corridor. Along to the fire door. I burst outside. The car was waiting, the engine running. The two men Foster had sent with us were sitting where we'd left them in the front. Knife Man was in the driving seat. I dived into the back of the car. Harry scrambled in after me.

'Where's Bradley?' I shouted.

'He was right behind me,' Harry said, wide-eyed.

We both turned to the fire door. Men in suits were streaming outside. One of them had his phone clamped to his ear. Another spotted us and started running towards our car. He drew out a gun and pointed it at Knife Man. There was no sign of Bradley.

Knife Man pressed on the gas as the man outside fired his gun. It glanced off the bonnet as we sped away. I stared out of the back window. The man who'd run towards us was standing in the street, still pointing his gun in our direction. We roared around a corner. The helipad was only streets away, but we couldn't possibly go straight there.

'We have to go back for Bradley,' I said. 'They must have caught him.'

'Or he fainted,' Harry said. 'He looked really ill.'

Knife Man shook his head. 'We can't get into a shooting match. Mr Foster's top priority was to avoid armed conflict.'

'But—' I started.

'Shut up!' Knife Man snapped.

I exchanged a glance with Harry. He looked as upset as I felt. I mean, Bradley was annoying and in league with Foster, of course. But on the other hand, he was just a kid who I was supposed to have been looking after.

And now I'd left him all alone.

21: Punishment

Foster was waiting for us at the helipad. Knife Man had rung ahead to tell him what had happened. I couldn't hear Foster's response, but as soon as I saw him I knew he was beyond furious that Bradley had been left behind.

After asking us to explain 'how the hell' we'd lost him, he ordered Harry and me into the helicopter that was waiting on the tarmac. Through the window we could see Foster yelling at the two men who'd driven us. I couldn't catch much of what he said, but it was obvious he was sending them back for Bradley. As the two men roared away in their car, Foster boarded the helicopter. He neither looked at nor spoke to Harry and me, simply told the pilot to get us out of here as soon as possible.

By the time we arrived back at the little apartment in Lovistov it was dark and I was exhausted. Nico and Ed were still in the living room where we'd left them. As Foster shoved us inside and locked the door behind us, the past few hours seemed like a dream.

And then – five minutes later – the door burst open again and everything turned into a nightmare.

The four of us had been sitting and talking about what had happened in low voices on the sofas. We still had no idea if Cal had managed to alert either the local police force or Fergus and Avery back in Australia. But even if he had, we knew none of them would have any idea we'd been taken to this apartment in Lovistov. Neither would Amy with whom Ed had managed, briefly, to make remote contact when we were still based at the castle.

As Foster and Jack came in, we all stood up. A tense silence fell as Foster looked round at each one of us in turn. He cleared his throat.

'We've heard that Bradley was taken, unconscious, to hospital,' he said.

'He said he wasn't well,' I said. 'He—'

'Leaving him behind was careless,' Foster interrupted in a soft tone that was all the more menacing for being quiet. 'I don't understand how it happened. I thought you were using your Medusa ability to protect all three of you.'

'She did,' Harry said quickly.

I nodded. 'Me and Harry were in front, Bradley behind . . . when we were running out of the building.' I thought back to Bradley's shaking hands and pale, clammy face. 'It all happened real fast.'

'And *you* didn't notice you'd left him behind either?' Foster glared at Harry.

Harry looked away. I shook my head. It was outrageous

for Foster to blame either me or Harry for Bradley's capture.

'People were chasing us,' I said, feeling my anger mounting. 'It was confusing. We were running fast and Bradley was ill before then anyway.' I drew myself up. 'If Bradley got taken, it's nobody's fault but yours.'

Foster glared at me. His grey eyes were like tiny stones, his lips pressed together in an expression of determined fury.

'How dare you blame me,' he said. His voice sent a shard of ice into me, but no way was I going to let him see how intimidated I felt.

'Of course I blame you, it's totally your fault,' I said, putting my hands on my hips and staring up at him. 'It's your fault because Bradley was scared. It's your fault because he was inexperienced. It's your fault because he wasn't well. *You* made him come with us in spite of all those things. On top of which, *you* gave him the Medusix in the first place.'

'That's probably what made him ill,' Nico added.

'No,' Foster insisted. 'It made him ill early on, but Bradley had fully recovered.'

'No, he hadn't,' I said. 'Everything that happened is *so* all your fault. You can't blame us.'

For a second, Foster looked so furious I thought he might explode. His face was a dark red colour and a vein pulsed at his temple.

'But I *do* blame you, Dylan.' Foster narrowed his eyes. 'In fact, I suspect you saw Bradley wasn't keeping up with you and left him on pur—' As he spoke, his phone rang. He held it to his ear, not taking his eyes off me. A second later he put it down again. 'My men inform me that Bradley is still unconscious.'

Silence fell. I was suddenly aware of Ed standing beside me and Harry and Nico opposite. They were all looking at me, the expressions on their faces part confusion, part terror.

Jack stepped forward, out of the shadows by the door. I'd forgotten he was even in the room.

'At least you know Bradley hasn't compromised the mission,' he said quietly to Foster. 'If he's unconscious, I mean.'

Jeez, I suddenly saw how frightened Jack himself was of Foster. The thought filled me with dread. Jack was rarely fazed by anything.

Foster ignored him. He was still staring at me.

And then he raised his gun and pointed it at my head.

'I'm afraid the truth is, Dylan ...' he said, cocking the gun, '... that where there's a crime there has to be a punishment.'

I looked down the barrel of the revolver. Was he going to shoot me? Because of Bradley? It didn't feel real.

Then I realised my legs were shaking.

I tried to engage my force field, but the Medutox being sprayed into the room had already reached me. I was defenceless.

'No.' Nico and Ed spoke together.

Harry strode towards me. He stood between me and Foster. 'You can't kill her,' he said.

Foster raised his eyebrows. 'I don't think any of you are in a position to tell me what to do.'

Jack walked forward, so he was right beside Foster. His eyes were on Foster's gun as he spoke.

'There's no need to take things this far,' he urged. 'The men can get Bradley out of hospital. He probably collapsed because ... well, it'll be just another side effect of the Medusix. I'm sure it will pass. So ... we'll get Bradley back. No one will know what the kids were doing in the conference rooms. They'll assume it was petty theft. No one will be looking for data that's been put *onto* a computer. The mission worked. Everything's going—'

'Shut up,' Foster ordered.

Jack stopped talking immediately, but he moved closer to Harry.

'Dylan had the power to save Bradley from capture and keep the mission on track,' Foster said softly. 'She failed. She must be punished.' He levelled his gun at me again. But Harry was still standing between us, blocking the shot. 'Get out of the way, Harry,' Foster ordered.

'No,' Harry said.

'Please,' Ed said, his voice practically hoarse with horror. 'Please, you can't shoot.'

Foster swung his gun round, pointing it now at Ed himself.

'I told you *not* to give me orders,' he barked. 'A punishment must be paid.' He paused. 'Still, Dylan remains a useful asset. And as Harry was also on the mission, he is also partly responsible for its failure.' He swivelled the gun back. 'So ... you're the one I'm going to kill, Harry.'

'No.' I put my hand out to protect him, forgetting again my Medusa power was completely gone.

'No, you can't.' Jack was on Harry's other side. 'Foster, this makes no sense. Harry's as useful as the others. I know he wasn't supposed to follow me out here, but he can hack into anything and—'

'. . . and it's murder,' Nico added.

Foster called out and Broken Nose came into the room.

'Move her,' Foster ordered, pointing at me.

Broken Nose strode over and pulled me away from Harry. He dragged me over to stand beside Nico and Ed.

'No,' I said. I kicked at the man's legs, but he jerked my arm behind my back. I winced with the pain.

Foster levelled his gun at Harry again. I forgot the pain in my arm. This was real. Foster meant it. He was about to shoot.

Harry knew it too. He turned to me. 'See ya, Red,' he said.

'No.' The voice that came out of me was broken and small – a voice I didn't even know I had. 'No, please.' I struggled against Broken Nose again but, again, he jerked on my arm. I stopped.

'Say goodbye to your son, Jack,' Foster sneered.

He pointed the gun. I stared at his fingers. They were squeezing the trigger. It was about to happen. There was nothing I could do to stop it.

'NO!' As I yelled, Foster fired.

And Jack leaped in front of the bullet.

22: The Sacrifice

The shot rang out. Jack crumpled to the ground. There was a terrible silence, then Harry let out an agonised roar and hurled himself at Foster. He landed a punch into Foster's guts. Caught by surprise, Foster bent double. Broken Nose let go of me and rushed over.

Harry was still kicking and punching and roaring his head off. Out of the corner of my eye I could see Nico – a blur – racing towards him and Foster. I darted over to Jack and knelt down beside him. His breath was coming in gasps. His hands were clutched over his belly, blood seeping through the fingers.

Jack was blinking, his eyes full of shock. He said something, but his voice was so faint I couldn't hear it. I leaned down closer, so my ear was right over his mouth.

'Pck,' he whispered.

'What?' I leaned in further.

'Pocket.' Jack's breathing was laboured and wheezy. It was clearly costing him everything to speak.

I looked up. Foster and Broken Nose were still fighting off Harry and Nico. Ed was standing behind me, watching. Jack saw him too. His eyes pleaded with us as he mouthed the word again.

Pocket.

I slid my hand into his shirt pocket. My fingers wrapped round a small plastic card. I pulled it out and tucked it swiftly into my own pocket.

As I turned back to Jack, he looked up at me. His eyes were the brightest of blues. Just like his son's.

'Save Harry.' The words were barely audible, but the look in his eyes said everything. 'Save Harry, please.'

'I will,' I whispered, bending over him again. 'I—'

But as I spoke, the pleading left Jack's eyes. And there was only a blankness.

I sat back. He was dead. Across the room, Nico was still fighting Broken Nose. Harry, on the other hand, had stopped struggling against Foster. He was staring down at his father's lifeless body, his face the colour of ash.

I stood up and Ed pulled me away from Jack's body as Foster strode over. Without speaking, he bent down and felt for Jack's pulse. Foster's shirt was torn where Harry had attacked him and his eyes still burned with fury, but his face was otherwise composed.

'Dead,' Foster said, looking up from Jack's body. He turned to Harry. 'Your father paid the punishment for you. You're luckier than you deserve.'

'You're a murderer.' The words shot out of me, fury rising

165

at the sight of Foster's cold, hard gaze. 'Nobody needed to die.'

Foster shrugged. 'Take it as a warning,' he said. 'Thanks to you we've had to move operations away from the castle – but we're getting more Medusix ready and soon we'll have more kids to test it on.' He turned to Broken Nose, still holding Nico. 'Get rid of the body.' And then he turned and stalked out of the room.

Broken Nose let Nico go and went over to Jack as another guard arrived. Together they picked the body up and took it away.

The door shut behind them. I looked around. Nico and Ed were staring at Harry, who sat on the couch, his head in his hands. I could see neither of them knew what to say to him.

It was up to me.

I went over, sat down beside Harry and put my hand on his back. He looked at me with haunted eyes. I slid my arm around his shoulders and squeezed his arm.

'I'm sorry,' I stammered.

Harry rubbed his cheek and blew out his breath.

'I'm sorry too, man.' Nico had walked over and was standing in front of us. He offered Harry a sympathetic smile.

Beside him, Ed nodded.

I looked at each of them in turn. 'Guys,' I said. 'We have to get out of here.'

'I know.' Nico sighed. 'But I don't see how. Foster has taken away our Medusa powers and—'

'It doesn't matter,' I interrupted. 'We'll just have to do it without them.' I pulled the card from my pocket. 'Jack wanted us to have this.'

Harry took the card from me. It was plain white plastic with a magnetic strip along one side. 'What is it?' he said.

'I don't know,' I admitted.

Harry turned the card over. Four numbers were printed in black marker pen on the other side: *5739*

'That's too short to be a phone number,' Nico said.

'It's got to be some kind of pin,' Ed said. 'Like for getting money out of the bank ...'

Harry weighed the card in his hand. 'My best guess ...' His voice cracked with emotion. He took a deep breath. 'I reckon this number must be today's code for the front door here. It's the only thing that makes sense.'

I nodded, remembering the keypad by the front door and how Harry had punched in numbers to let us out before.

Ed rubbed his forehead. He lowered his voice. 'You mean this number could get us out of here.'

'Yes, I think so,' Harry said miserably. 'Jack knew you'd all been sprayed, so Nico's telekinesis wouldn't work. This pin number's our only option.'

I stared at him. 'So if we can just overpower Foster and the guards, we can let ourselves out of the apartment?'

'Exactly.' Harry paused. He stared down at the card itself. 'But I don't know what *this* is for.'

I looked back at the piece of white plastic that the pin number was written on.

167

'Maybe it was just the place where Jack wrote the code down?' I suggested.

'Maybe.' Harry looked away.

'Or maybe it means something significant ... we just don't know what yet,' Ed suggested.

'Maybe Jack was trying to help us, before he ...' Nico tailed off.

We fell silent. Harry bowed his head. He put down the card, as if he couldn't bear to look at it any more. I exchanged a look with Nico. Ed wandered across the room to the locked window.

'D'you think that could be true, Red?' Harry's voice was strained. 'D'you think Dad was trying to help us escape? I mean, he knew what Foster was planning ... he knew that our lives were in danger.'

There was a pause. To be honest I had no idea what Jack had been up to, but that wasn't what Harry needed to hear. 'I'm sure Jack was trying to help us,' I said. 'The last thing he said was ... was about wanting you to be safe.'

Harry bit his lip. I picked up the card. I had no idea how to offer Harry any comfort through what I said. Maybe the best thing I could do right now was focus on the practicalities of our next challenge.

'Let's get ready,' I said. 'As soon as the next guard comes in, we overpower him. Agreed?'

Nico and Harry nodded.

'Er ... wouldn't it make sense to wait until Foster

leaves the apartment – or at least sends some of the guards away?' Ed said from the window across the room.

'How will we know when he does?' Nico asked.

Ed pointed out of the window. 'I can just see his big car from here,' he said. 'It's parked in the alley.'

'Good, we'll take it in turns to keep watch,' I said. 'As soon as we see the car go, we use the next opportunity to escape.'

The next opportunity came quicker than any of us were expecting. Ed had agreed to take the first watch. Nico was lying on one of the couches, asleep. I had been sitting beside Harry on the other. We didn't say much and, after a while, my eyes closed.

I awoke with a start. Harry was shaking my shoulder. 'Ed says Foster's just driven off in his car. He had Broken Nose with him.'

I sat up, rubbing my eyes. Ed and Nico were standing by the other couch, talking in low voices.

I looked up at Harry. There were dark shadows under his eyes – it didn't look like he'd got any sleep at all.

'If Foster's taken Broken Nose, that means there's only one guard left here,' I whispered.

'I know.' Harry turned to the others. 'Ready?'

Nico and Ed nodded.

I stood up, my heart thudding. 'Nico and Harry on either side of the door?' I said. 'Ed and me yelling?'

'You took the words out of my mouth,' Nico said with a terse grin.

The boys took up their positions. I stood beside Ed, opposite the door and beside the side lamp that was the only source of light in the room. 'Go!' I said.

Ed yelled. I screamed. Nico and Harry banged on the door. Seconds later the guard appeared. As he opened the door fully, I yanked the light out from its socket.

The guard shouted as Nico and Harry jumped him. I could just make out their silhouettes against the light from the hall. I ran across to join them. The guard was already on the floor. Nico was binding his hands. Ed and I wound the lamp wire round his ankles.

'Come on!' Harry was already in the doorway.

I followed him through. Nico came after. Ed stopped to lock the door behind us, then we raced to the front door. My heart was in my mouth as I punched in the numbers from the white plastic card. I handed it to Nico and pushed at the door.

With a click, the door opened. The four of us rushed through and across the landing to the stairs. We hurtled down the steps and out through the side exit.

It was raining outside and the pavement of the deserted alley shone in the street lamps.

'Which way?' I gasped.

We were clearly in a different part of Lovistov from the area close to the church where we'd first arrived. Nico pocketed the card and pointed towards the busy street just visible at the end of the alley.

'Down there,' he said. 'We need to get as far away from

here as we can. In half an hour we'll get our powers back. Then Ed can hopefully contact Cal or K—'

He stopped. I knew he'd been about to say Ketty's name. His face contorted with pain.

So much loss. And all because my dad had been a genius and synthesised a gene for psychic abilities. For the first time, I wished that the Medusa gene – and the drug Medusix that mimicked its effects – had never been created.

'We need to move.' I led the way along the alley. We emerged onto the busy street. Rain pattered onto our heads and shoulders, as we sped across the road and on past shops with glass windows and dark-painted doors, and homes with lace curtains revealing lights and families inside.

On we ran. As we raced along, Harry took my hand and I found myself wishing we were just an ordinary boy and girl, out for the evening with our friends. Not part of a bizarre group of teenage freaks whose lives were destined always to lead to trouble, misery and death.

At last – just as the rain slowed to a drizzle – we stopped running. We had reached a small kids' playground – swings and a roundabout. It was dark and deserted, the only light coming from a street lamp over twenty metres away.

Ed leaned against the roundabout. I sat down on one of the swings.

Harry slumped into the seat beside me.

'It'll be over soon,' I said to him, forcing a smile onto my face. 'We'll make contact with the others and we'll pay Foster back. I promise. Then it will all be over. We'll be free.'

But inside I couldn't see how – even if we stopped Foster – we would ever be truly free. Not while the Medusa gene still exerted its power over us.

23: Plan of Attack

It was dawn. And freezing. Harry, Ed, Nico and I were hiding out round the back of a run-down warehouse, taking it in turns to keep watch. Ed had made contact with Cal about an hour ago. He wasn't far away and – much to our relief – he was with Fergus Fox and Avery Jones.

He had explained, via Ed, that when he took Tania to a local police station so she could be returned to her family, he'd been held for questioning himself. *That* was why he hadn't returned to the lake earlier.

Still, I wasn't interested in the details of what Cal had been doing. All that mattered was that he and the adults were on their way.

Harry, Ed and Nico were huddled and shivering against the warehouse wall. It was my turn to keep watch but it was too cold to stand still. I wandered across the street and found myself in a small square. It was kind of pretty – with trees round the sides and a cute stone fountain in the middle. I walked diagonally across the square to a stone block by the fountain. It was a war memorial – very abstract and modern, made of overlapping angular carvings. These things always fascinate me. Erected to honour dead soldiers, I wondered who else had stood, looking at the same statue, mourning a loss.

I thought back to my parents. Both dead within months of my birth. At least they had loved each other. At least I had that. Jack hadn't really loved Harry's mom, Laura. I wasn't sure he'd really cared about Harry all that much, until he died to save Harry's life.

Footsteps echoed behind me, loud on the paving squares. I turned round, instantly alert, and peered past the war memorial. A red-haired girl was crossing the square. She clearly hadn't spotted me behind the statue. She looked somehow familiar. An uneasy feeling crept down my spine. And then the girl turned round.

I gasped. It was like a punch to the guts. Red hair. Green eyes. Long legs. My own reflection stared back at me.

Except ... my brain resisted what my eyes were telling me. For a start, there was no mirror. Plus the 'Dylan' in front of me looked different. This wasn't a reflection where the features are transposed to the other side of the face ... it was me ... how I looked to others, only wearing different clothes.

I stared at myself. No nose piercing. And I would *never* wear a scarf that shade of orange. Which left only one explanation.

'*Amy?*' I said.

As I spoke, she changed, the hair darkening and shortening and the whole body shrinking down into itself. A second later Ed's sister was herself again. She looked up at me with big, worried eyes.

'Sorry, Dylan ...' she stammered. 'I was practising in case ...' She tailed off.

I blinked, still thrown by what had happened. I shook myself.

'Cal didn't mention you were coming with him,' I said. 'Where is he? Where are the others?'

Amy pointed across the square. Ed, Harry and Nico were emerging from our hiding place. Avery Jones and Fergus Fox stood on either side of them, Cal to one side. I looked over at the two men. Fergus was, as usual, dressed in his teacher-type clothes. Everything a bit shapeless and worn. He was tall, of course, but Avery was taller. Almost bald, with his remaining hair close-cropped and wearing a sharp designer suit. The two men were about the same age, but worlds apart in terms of dress sense and personality.

At the sight of the two men, something released inside me. A sob rose in my chest – after the past few days of stress and fear, at last we were safe. Amy was gazing at me thoughtfully.

'Are you all right, Dylan?' she said.

The timid kindness in her voice irritated me. Who was Amy to feel sorry for me?

'I'd be a lot better if you weren't here,' I snarled.

Amy looked crestfallen.

For a second, I could hear Ketty's voice in my head. *Why d'you have to be so rude, Dylan?* I shook myself, not wanting to acknowledge the wave of grief washing over me. Since when did I care so much about Ketty?

The others walked up. Uncle Fergus put his hand on my shoulder. 'I'm so sorry,' he said. 'Cal told us about Ketty.'

Tears were pricking at my eyes. I forced them back.

'I thought you'd be mad at us,' I grunted.

'Oh, we are,' Avery said. I followed his gaze to Nico, but Nico's expression was blank. There was no trace of the pain I knew he was feeling over Ketty – he had that buried deep again.

At least Nico's biological father – Avery – and his step-father – Fergus – were here now. Avery's presence reinforced the fact that Cal was Nico's half-brother, while Fergus, being my uncle, was a reminder that I was Nico's cousin.

All of which, I guessed, made us family.

Jeez, listen to me. I'd be bawling in a minute.

'First things first,' Fergus said briskly. 'We've hired two cars and our rented house is about thirty minutes away. Let's get you back there and warm and fed.'

As we headed for the two cars, I looked around for Harry. He was behind me and smiled as I caught his eye.

'When we get in the car, you're sitting next to me, Red,' he said.

'Oh am I?' I said, feeling secretly pleased.

Nico gave a snort. 'Puke-a-rama,' he said.

I glared at him. How dare he talk like that after Harry's father had just died. But Harry just gave Nico a thump on the back.

'You wish,' he said.

Nico offered up a hollow chuckle. I shook my head. Boys and their banter . . . I didn't get it. At least they were trying to act normally, I supposed.

Ed and Amy were already in the back seat. They were arguing in hushed voices about Amy being here.

'But I don't understand why they brought you,' Ed was saying.

'Because Fergus and Avery thought I could be useful,' Amy protested.

The door shut behind them. Cal was already sitting next to Avery up front in the other car. Harry and I got in behind them. Harry put his arm round me and I leaned against his shoulder.

I must have fallen asleep – deeply asleep – because when I woke up I was in bed, still dressed, but tucked into crisp cotton sheets that smelled of soap powder.

I opened my eyes. I was in a simply furnished room with cream walls and lemon-coloured curtains hanging at the window. The curtains were drawn open and a bright sun was visible through the glass, high in the sky.

The single bed across the room was empty, but unmade. From the crumpled pink pyjamas and bright orange scarf on the sheets, I was guessing that was where Amy was sleeping.

I got up. I felt a bit achy, but otherwise fine – though I

177

was starving hungry. I went out of the bedroom and found myself on a landing. Through the open doors around me I could see there were two other bedrooms and a bathroom. None of them were occupied, but excited voices were drifting up from the ground floor. I made my way down the stairs. The whole house was like the bedroom I'd woken up in – neat and clean and plainly furnished with cream walls throughout and functional wooden furniture.

The stairs brought me to an open-plan living area. I could see through to a kitchen at one end, where Nico, Ed, Cal and Harry were all sitting at a table talking loudly.

'Hi, Dylan.' It was Amy. I hadn't noticed her before. She was sitting, curled up on the huge couch opposite the fireplace. As I looked over, she smiled.

'Hey, it's Princess Ten-Faces,' I said, in a not-unfriendly way.

Amy's smile seemed to freeze into place. 'Er ... we're sharing a room,' she said.

I rolled my eyes. 'Awesome.' What did she want? A prize? I strode past her, making for the boys in the kitchen. As I went in, Harry got up and came over. He put his arm round my shoulders.

Nico whispered something in Cal's ear. Cal looked up at us and stifled a laugh.

Jeez, they were *sooo* immature.

'Okay, Red?' Harry asked. 'You've like been asleep for hours.'

'I'm good.' I leaned in closer and kissed him.

Harry beamed. At the table Ed was blushing a deep red, while Cal stared at me with his mouth gaping.

Nico raised his eyebrows. 'Wow, you *are* loved-up, Dilly,' he said.

I stared at him. Nico's eyes were blank, but he wasn't fooling me. He might sound all hard and cool, but I could see he was hurting. Still, if everyone was trying to behave normally, I might as well join in.

'Don't call me Dilly,' I snapped. I took Harry's hand and led him back to the table. We sat down next to each other. 'I heard you talking from upstairs. What's going on?'

'Harry's just hacked into one of Foster's accounts,' Ed said. 'We've found out where he's holding the children he's recruited *and* where he's transferred all the stuff from the castle lab.'

I smiled at Harry who pinked a little.

'It's a complex about five miles away,' he said.

'Fergus and Avery have gone out for supplies,' Nico added. 'We've just been working out the best way to get into this complex. It looks mega-secure.'

Harry nodded. 'There's an outer gate plus CCTV and alarms and guards ...'

'You mean Fergus and Avery are going to let us go in alone?' I said, surprised.

Cal and Nico exchanged glances.

'No, they're coming too,' Cal explained.

'They didn't want us to go into the complex at all,' Nico said. 'But we have to stop Foster developing Medusix.'

179

Ed nodded. 'We can't let him use it on those children he's trying to turn into a hit squad.'

'And we have to pay him back for Ketty,' Nico said.

There was a long silence, then Cal cleared his throat. 'We don't want the authorities to find out we're here, so we're going to have to be careful.'

'The authorities wouldn't be much help even if they knew. We're the only ones who can get past Foster's security without him realising,' Nico said grimly. 'We're going to need all our skills.'

'Especially mine,' Amy said from the doorway.

I looked up and gasped. She had transformed herself into Foster.

Ed shook his head.

'Meet our secret weapon,' Nico said.

I tilted my head to one side. 'Not bad, Ten-Faces,' I said. 'But you need to look meaner.'

'Like this?' Amy scowled. She did look remarkably like Foster.

'Awesome,' I said.

Amy/Foster grinned.

Ed shook his head again. 'Even if Amy's impression gets us through the first security gate, there are plenty of other places where we could be stopped and discovered,' he said.

'Then we better go prepared,' I said. 'What's the plan?'

24: Getting In

We travelled in separate cars until we reached a spot about two hundred metres from Foster's new complex. It was in the middle of nowhere, a sprawling single-storey building made of white concrete and surrounded by a barbed wire fence and then open countryside.

We stopped the cars on the edge of the trees and got out. The sun was fading in the sky and, already, bright lights were illuminating the outline of the complex. As Harry's hacking had discovered, there was absolutely no way to approach the building without being seen. We had to go in through the security gate which was set into the fence just half a mile further down this road.

We clustered around Avery Jones as he went over our plan one last time.

'Okay, Amy,' he said at last. 'Time to transform.'

Amy nodded nervously. She was already wearing one of Avery's old suits with the trousers rolled up. She had her own shoes – plain, brown loafers – but they would barely show under the trousers.

As she closed her eyes and focused on becoming a Foster lookalike, Uncle Fergus spoke to the rest of us.

'Remember, the plan is to stay in two groups of four,' he said.

I exchanged a look with Nico. Fergus and Avery had insisted that one adult should accompany three of us each. *As if they're looking after us*, Nico had muttered earlier.

'We know the plan,' I said, feeling slightly irritated. Fergus was a good, kind, straightforward man – but he was also overprotective and prone to worry about details that just weren't important.

'I know you know.' Fergus sighed. 'My point is that once we're inside, things can go wrong and in the chaos of the conflict all sorts of unforeseen challenges may come up.'

I shook my head. Did he seriously think we didn't know that? Still, maybe I should try and reassure him.

'Well, before, when we had Ketty, even when we knew what was going to happen – which I guess wasn't often – it didn't always help. I mean, it didn't need to. We're good at thinking on our feet.'

There was an awkward silence. Nico glared at me.

Jeez, I hadn't meant anything … I was just making a point about how experienced we all were. *Surely* Nico didn't think I was putting down Ketty's Medusa ability?

I blushed, remembering the many occasions on which I'd done so.

'I didn't mean it wasn't useful sometimes,' I mumbled. 'Ketty's gift was cool.'

'I want you to be careful,' Fergus went on, ignoring me. 'Don't waste time looking at Foster's experiments and research. Just concentrate on destroying it all.'

'Can we get on with this?' Nico said rather sharply.

I glanced at him. There were lines around his eyes and his normally smooth olive skin was sallow, almost grey. It struck me that he'd been looking like that for a while now – since he'd heard about Ketty. It's funny, if you'd asked me a week ago, I'd have said that Nico was fond of her, but that the relationship wasn't really that serious – at least from his point of view. But the last day had proved to me that Nico was hurting almost more than he could bear.

'Well, I'm ready.' We all turned to look at Amy.

It was an amazing transformation – even better than in the kitchen earlier. Tall and male, with her suit trousers now rolled down, she looked at us with cold grey eyes. It was impossible to tell that she wasn't Foster.

'Okay,' Avery said briskly. 'Team A into the first car.' He pulled on a leather jacket that was supposed to make him look like one of Foster's men. Having met some of them, I knew that Avery was simply too groomed to be really convincing – but hopefully the security checkpoint guards would only give him a cursory glance. Avery got into the driver's seat and opened the door for Amy – as Foster – to sit beside him. Fergus bound my hands loosely behind my back while Nico did the same for Harry. It would be easy enough to slip off these ropes when we needed to. The point was to get us through the checkpoint looking like Foster's prisoners.

As I scrambled into the back seat after Harry, Fergus gave my shoulder an anxious squeeze.

'Be careful,' he said.

'We'll be fine,' I said. I guess losing Ketty must have really shaken him up, but surely Fergus realised we'd been going on challenging missions just like this for the past six months. I had my Medusa power back. I could extend my force field around everyone in seconds if the need arose.

Avery drove off. He took the bumpy track slowly, coming to a stop at the security gate. Close to, we could all see there were two men inside the checkpoint hut, both dressed in smart blue uniforms. Neither were visibly armed, but knowing Foster I was sure both were carrying guns.

Ed appeared in my head. *How many guards?* he thought-spoke.

Two guards. Concealed weapons, I replied.

Thanks. Ed broke the connection. He was waiting with the others around the corner. He, Nico and the rest of the second team would distract and capture the men at the checkpoint ... after Amy – in disguise as Foster – had got Avery, Harry and me inside the building.

One of the checkpoint guards sauntered over as Avery wound down his window. The guard peered into the car.

'Evening, sir,' he said to Amy. He glanced over his

shoulder at me and Harry in the back seat. 'Do you want me to take the new kids in for you?'

'Er . . . no thanks,' Amy said.

I froze. Her voice wasn't low enough. And she sounded too hesitant and polite. The real Foster would have barked out his refusal.

The man seemed to sense something wasn't quite right too.

'Are you sure, sir?' he said, an ingratiating tone to his voice. 'I took the last lot inside. I know where they go.'

Amy was now turning red in the face. For goodness' sake. I dug my knee into the back of her seat. She needed to get a grip.

Unfortunately the checkpoint guard spotted what I was doing.

'Need me to teach this one a lesson, sir?' he asked, jerking his head in my direction.

'There's nothing you could teach me except how to be an idiot,' I snapped, the words flying out of me before I could bite them back.

Amy said nothing. *No.* Now the guard looked really startled, not just at my outburst but at Foster's lack of reaction.

I caught Harry's eye. *No, no, no.* Everything was going wrong, even before we'd begun.

There was a moment of tense silence. Amy was still silent – and bright red in the face. Any second now the guard was going to guess this wasn't really Foster. I had to do something to make him believe it was. And fast.

185

'You're all a bunch of losers,' I snarled. 'Especially *you*, Foster.' I prodded my elbow into the back of Amy's seat again. Hopefully she would realise I was deliberately trying to provoke her – to give her a reason to get angry and to show her – or, rather, Foster's – temper in action.

Another second passed, then Amy took the bait.

'Shut up!' She made her hand a fist and swiped it across my face.

I engaged my force field just in time, so the blow brushed over me like a breeze. I pretended to reel away, howling in pain.

'Stop it!' Harry's yell sounded completely authentic.

I held my breath. Had Amy's display of violence convinced the guard she was Foster?

'Get out of the way!' Amy shouted at the guard. 'Your job is to stay here, not chaperone kids into the complex.'

I looked up. Chastened, the guard was backing away from the car, waving us through. Avery revved the engine and we drove off. As he wound up the window again, Amy gave a sigh of relief.

'That was close,' she said. 'I didn't hurt you, did I, Dylan?'

'No,' I snapped. 'And don't relax just yet. There's still a long way to go.'

We reached the front of the complex. Amy drew herself up and rapped on the door. Another guard in a blue uniform opened it.

'Take these two to join the other kids,' Amy ordered. She sounded cold and hard, just like Foster.

'Yes, sir.' The guard nodded and led me and Harry away, along a bleak concrete corridor. Everything was in motion. Amy and Avery were going to try and get to the communications nerve centre of the building while Nico and the others dealt with the checkpoint. My job – and Harry's – was to rescue the hit squad children. I gripped the ends of the rope that was still wound loosely around my wrists. I had to hope that the guards didn't spot it wasn't properly tied.

The guard ushered us down a narrow flight of steps and into a basement room. It was as bleak and cold as the rest of the building – empty apart from another guard who sat in front of a row of computers.

I peered at the screens. There were four computers altogether, all showing pictures from webcams trained on different rooms. One revealed the room we were in now. The next two showed bleak-looking cells, both containing two low camp beds and a child of about ten or eleven sitting on each one. These must be the kids Foster had conned into his hit squad. I exchanged a look with Harry. Now all we had to do was work out exactly where those rooms were – and somehow get to the kids inside them.

The guard prodded my shoulder. 'This way,' he said.

As I turned to follow Harry, I caught sight of the fourth computer on the end of the row. I stopped, stunned by what I was looking at. The guard prodded me. I had to walk on, but my head was spinning.

Surely what I'd seen wasn't – *couldn't* be – true.

Could it?

NICO

25: Checkpoint

We waited around the corner, under cover of some trees. Ed had just made contact with Dylan and we knew there were two guards at the checkpoint, each armed with a concealed weapon. I turned to Fergus. My stepdad was wearing an anxious frown. It struck me, not for the first time, that Fergus really wasn't cut out for this kind of mission. He belonged in a school, where the biggest conflicts he'd ever get involved in would be arguments with rebellious students over doing homework on time or the proper wearing of their school uniforms.

Military-style rescue operations weren't his thing. And yet here he was, trying to help us do what we needed to do in order to save the children Foster had recruited to his hit squad and prevent him from developing the Medusix drug.

'Are you all right?' I asked him.

Fergus looked at me, startled. 'Yes, er ...' He turned to Ed. 'Shouldn't you be attempting to contact Dylan or Amy yet?'

I knew he was worrying about not having a more tradi-tional way of keeping in touch, anxious about relying on Ed's ability to communicate through remote telepathy.

'We agreed five minutes,' Ed said patiently. 'I have to give them time to get past the checkpoint. If they find me in their heads while they're in the middle of dealing with Foster's guards, it might put them off their stride.' He paused. 'Especially Amy.'

I sighed. Ed was still really unhappy that the rest of us had insisted Amy be allowed to join us on this mission. I could understand why he was protective of her, but the truth was Amy had an amazing Medusa skill. Her ability to appear identical to Foster himself was the single biggest advantage over Foster's men we had – and the best option for getting her, Avery, Harry and Dylan inside the complex without anyone suspecting our plan to rescue Foster's latest hit squad recruits and blow up the lab.

We stood in silence for a few more minutes. Cal was hov-ering above the ground. I'd noticed he deployed his ability to fly like that whenever he was nervous. Not that Cal would admit he was scared.

As I glanced again at Ed, his expression took on that far-away look he gets when he's communicating telepathically with someone.

He blinked, presumably breaking the connection.

'Ed?'

'It's Amy,' he said. 'She says everything's going to plan. Dylan and Harry have been taken off to the hit squad kids and she and Avery are heading for the comms centre now. The guards were completely convinced she was Foster.'

He turned away, making remote contact again.

'Goodness, that's such a lot for Amy to deal with,' Fergus said, a fretful edge to his voice.

'She'll be fine,' I said. 'Once she's got to the communications centre and ordered the alarm system to be disabled, we'll be able to get through no problem.'

'I still don't see why I can't just fly us in,' Cal grunted.

I rolled my eyes. 'We've been over this,' I said. 'If anyone spots us in the air, we'll be open targets. Even though we know Foster and the Lovistov guards aren't here right now, his other men are bound to be fully aware of our Medusa skills. They'll be on alert as it is.'

'Not long now,' Ed said. 'Amy says they're almost at the comms centre. She's going to give me the directions to the lab as soon as she and Avery can work out where it is.'

Another silence fell. I tried to keep my focus on the job in hand. The rest of the mission was a huge challenge: while Amy and Avery disabled the alarms and Harry and Dylan found Foster's hit squad recruits, the rest of us had to try and reach the lab area. This was bound to be the most thoroughly guarded part of the complex and I was going to need all my strength and nerve to get us there and destroy it, especially as things stood – with Cal feeling disgruntled about us not making more use of his flying ability, Fergus looking downright terrified and Ed all distracted with worry over Amy.

However, even as I tried to force myself to go over the plan again, my thoughts – as they had done so often in the past couple of days – went to Ketty. It was the same thing as usual ... I'd manage not to think about her for maybe a minute or two at a time. Then the memories – and the pain – came flooding back, worse than ever. The same three questions kept circling my head like vultures.

How could she be dead?

How could the world carry on without her in it?

How would I survive?

There were no answers to these questions. Just a horrible dark hollow feeling in my head and my guts when I asked them.

'Okay.' Ed's voice interrupted my thoughts. 'Amy says that they can't turn off the communication link to the checkpoint from inside the complex.'

'Oh no.' Fergus's eyes widened with alarm. 'But we *have* to get past those guards. And ... and Avery said they were armed ...'

I glanced at Cal. It was kind of funny hearing an adult get so worked up about something that really wasn't going to be a problem. Cal grinned back at me.

'It's cool,' I said. 'Let's go.'

We crept through the trees until we were directly behind the checkpoint hut. Cal took hold of Ed's wrist on one side and Fergus's on the other. He caught my eye.

'Just in case,' he said.

I nodded. The last thing we wanted was to draw attention

to ourselves but it was good that Cal could get the others away from the scene in seconds, if need be.

'Okay.' Ed broke his mind-reading connection. 'Amy says the CCTV showing the checkpoint is down. You can go, Nico.'

I darted away from the others, running right up to the edge of the checkpoint hut. I focused on the barbed wire fence that stretched along the boundary of the complex. Then I used my telekinesis to raise a large branch from the ground opposite and hurled it against the fence. It crashed against the wire mesh, then thudded to the ground.

'What was that?' said one of the guards inside the hut.

As he spoke, more noises sounded from behind the hut – created, I knew, by Cal, Fergus and Ed. Our plan was to divide the two guards, to make it easier for us to deal with them.

I raised the branch telekinetically and flung it against the fence again.

Footsteps from inside. Both guards appeared. One immediately sped round to the back of the hut investigating the sound that had come from that direction. The other stood where he was, staring at the branch I'd thrown. There was no wind in the air – it was a still, calm evening – and he was obviously wondering how the branch had travelled to the fence. He reached inside his jacket and drew out a gun.

Gotcha.

With a swift flick of my wrist, I tugged the gun out of

his hand. It was simple, mostly because he wasn't expecting it.

I tossed the gun high in the sky, then flung it far out into the woods beyond the complex. The guard spun round, his eyes wide with panic. He reached for his radio. With another firm flick, I wrenched both the handset and the receiver off his belt and flung them in the opposite direction. The guard staggered backwards. He opened his mouth to yell out. Before he could make a sound, I picked him telekinetically off the ground and sent him round to the back of the hut. He whirled through the air. I followed after. The others were running towards us. I could just see the second guard, bound and gagged, behind them. I smiled as I ran. Ed had obviously managed to hold the man's mind long enough for Cal and Fergus to tie him up. I set my guard down in front of them. Immediately Ed made eye contact and the guard froze. Fergus whipped out a pair of handcuffs, while Cal bound the man's ankles.

Fergus tied a gag round the man's mouth. As I ran up, Cal pushed the guard to the ground. He shrank away, clearly in a state of complete shock.

'Sorted,' Cal said with a grin.

'Like taking sweets off a couple of toddlers,' I said, grinning back.

'That's all very well, but those men had proper guns,' Fergus said disapprovingly. 'Any one of you could have been seriously hurt.'

Ignoring him, I turned to Ed. He was gazing into space, clearly attempting remote telepathy once more.

'Come on,' I urged. 'Has Amy told you where the labs are yet? We need to get there as fast as possible.'

'Wait.' Ed held up his hand. He looked worried.

I rolled my eyes. Honestly, he was as big a fusspot as Fergus.

Cal's eyes were shining. 'That was awesome, bro,' he said.

'I know,' I said. 'Everything's going totally to plan. This mission's going to be a breeze.'

'No it's not.' Ed turned to me, white-faced. 'I can't make contact with Amy.'

I stared at him. 'Are you sure?' I said. 'Maybe she's just focusing on being Foster . . . maybe—?'

'No.' Ed shook his head to underline his point. 'No, you don't understand. I think she's been sprayed with Medutox.'

'But that means—' I looked at him in horror.

'That means she's been found out,' Ed said.

A tense silence fell over us.

I gritted my teeth. 'Then we have to go in and get her back,' I said. 'Come on. We'll find the labs after.' And without looking to see if the others followed, I set off through the gate towards the complex.

26: Finding Amy

I crept past the gate. The CCTV camera at the front of the complex was positioned just above the front door, about twenty metres directly ahead of me.

Cal, Ed and Fergus raced over.

'Let me fly us in,' Cal said. 'It's a flat roof. Maybe there'll be a door down to the main part of the building from there. If not, I can fly us off.'

I hesitated. It was a risk – Cal's flying was likely to attract attention. On the other hand, if the CCTV showing the front of the building wasn't disabled, then we wouldn't stand a chance trying to get inside by breaking a window or attempting to storm in through the front door.

'I don't like this,' Fergus said. 'It sounds really dangerous.'

'Cal's excellent in the air,' I said. 'He can fly us in and out super fast. I think it's a good plan.' As I said the words, it occurred to me that if Ketty were here, we wouldn't need a plan – she'd be able to see into the near future for us. I met Ed's eyes and knew he was thinking the same thing.

198

A beat passed. The pain weighed like a stone in the pit of my stomach.

'Well,' Ed said with a sigh. 'I hate to agree with any proposal that involves flying but Cal's right. It's the only option.'

'Why don't we go in through the ground floor?' Fergus asked.

I looked over at the complex. 'Because all the entry points there are under surveillance. We're too vulnerable. We'll be seen and captured.'

'I'm not sure we should be going in at all,' Fergus added. 'It's too risky. Perhaps we should wait until Ed manages to make contact with Amy?'

I stared at him. 'If Amy's been sprayed, that isn't going to happen. Ed's really good at remote telepathy. If Amy was reachable, he'd be able to reach her.'

'Well, what about Dylan?' Fergus insisted, a frown creasing his forehead. 'Try contacting her. See if she knows what's going on.'

'I have,' Ed said patiently. 'I can't reach either of them.'

'We can't wait,' I said.

'No.' Ed nodded his agreement. 'We have to go after Amy.'

Fergus opened his mouth to protest again, but I grabbed Cal's wrist.

'Fly us onto the roof,' I said.

Cal reached for Ed's wrist. The three of us stood in line. Fergus took a step back.

'Let's just wait a second and think this through,' he said.

Cal and Ed both looked at me.

'There's no time,' I said.

'But—' Fergus started.

'Fly!' I ordered.

Cal zoomed high into the sky, Ed and I on either side of him. The wind rushed past my face and I had that exciting, slightly off-balance feeling of leaving my stomach behind on the ground. In seconds we had soared so far off the ground that Fergus was just a tiny dot below us and the complex like a toy building.

'We shouldn't leave Fergus,' Ed said, looking past Cal towards me.

'No choice,' I said. 'He's too hesitant. He's not cut out for missions. Having him with us risks everything. For him. For us. And for the others.'

Cal whooshed us across the sky. We were now hovering directly above the complex. I looked down. *Yes*, there was a raised structure on the flat roof ... with a door that must lead below.

'Put us down,' I said to Cal.

Seconds later we'd landed on the roof beside the door. Immediately I released Cal's wrist and studied the door. It appeared to contain at least three different kinds of locks. A metal padlock – that would be easy to spring open – plus an electronic bar *and* an alarmed laser field.

My heart sank. It was going to take all my skill and experience to get through those last two locks, especially the laser field – I'd never faced anything like it before. I twisted my wrist and released the padlock. That, at least, was straightforward. Ed pushed at the door but of course it was still shut fast.

'This is going to take some time,' I said through gritted teeth. 'I need to visualise the two locks on this door and they're both state of the art.'

'What about the card Jack gave us?' Ed asked. 'Maybe it's a key card for opening doors.'

'Maybe, but it won't work on this door.' I shook my head. 'It doesn't use that kind of system.'

'Try it anyway,' Cal urged.

I took the card out of my pocket and let Cal wave it around the frame of the door but, as I'd suspected, the door stayed shut.

Cal made a face. 'This sucks,' he said, handing the card back to me.

'I know.' I focused on the lock again. 'Give me some space, okay?'

Cal and Ed retreated a couple of metres across the roof and sat down. I carried on trying to visualise the electronic bar and the laser system. Thoughts of Ketty kept creeping into my mind again. The stone at the pit of my stomach weighed heavier than ever.

I told myself I should be concentrating on dealing with the people who were still alive: Amy and Avery and Dylan and Harry. Each one of them was important to me. In spite of her sharp tongue, Dylan was a good friend – and what I'd seen of Harry so far made me sure he would become one. Amy was a sweet kid and as for Avery ... well, I'd only recently found out Avery was my biological father. We still had a lot of catching up to do.

They were all important to me. So why was it Ketty who still filled my thoughts? Ketty ... whose image in my mind threatened to distract me from my focus on this door in front of me ... Ketty, who I missed so much that it hurt.

Ten minutes passed. Then fifteen. I turned away, taking a break. Cal and Ed looked anxiously on. I turned back to the door and tried again. Something in the door released – the electronic bar, I thought – but it still wouldn't open. 'Nearly there,' I muttered.

Time ticked away until we'd been on the roof for almost twenty-five minutes. From where we were standing it was impossible to make out the guards, still tied up behind the checkpoint, and though we could see the gate, Fergus was no longer in sight.

I was desperately aware that anyone – Foster or one of his Lovistov men – could turn up at any moment. As soon as they found the guards we'd tied up, our cover would be blown. That's if it wasn't blown already, with Ed still unable to reach the others inside.

As I turned to focus on the door again, footsteps sounded on the other side.

I froze. Cal grabbed my arm. He was already in flight, Ed on his other side. We zoomed around the jutting structure on the roof, hiding behind the wall to the side of the door.

I held my breath as the door opened. Cal kept his hand on my arm, poised to whisk us all into the air again if needed. I tensed myself, ready to disarm whoever was there.

A slow, single footstep across the flat roof. And then Dylan's face peered round the wall.

I lowered my hand. Cal released my arm.

'Dylan?' I said.

'They've got Amy,' she whispered. 'Come on, follow me.'

'How did you know we were here?' I said.

'Sssh.' Dylan put her finger to her lips, then beckoned us after her.

Ed, Cal and I followed her around the wall and through the door that had proved so hard for me to open.

Dylan crept on ahead. She had wrapped a blanket over her shoulders which seemed odd – though it was certainly cold in here. Down a flight of winding concrete steps. Something was wrong. Something to do with Dylan and that blanket. We reached the bottom step. Through another door into a white corridor. Round a bend . . . and then everything happened at once.

Dylan ducked. Two guards appeared out of nowhere. Before I could move or speak, one pointed his gun at my face. The other sprayed me with Medutox, then pulled me towards him, reaching to spray Ed who was right behind me.

As Cal was captured straight after, I glanced over at Dylan. She was being sprayed too. Straightaway she started changing . . . transforming . . . her dark red hair fading to brown ... her body shortening and fleshing out ... until Amy stood there. In tears. She dropped the blanket and I could see that, underneath it, she was still dressed in Avery's suit, with the trouser legs rolled up.

'I'm sorry, Nico,' she said. 'They made me do it. They've got Avery. They're going to kill him if we don't do what they say.'

27: Breathe and Focus

Amy was still apologising as the guards ushered us along another corridor and into a side room. Bare and windowless, the door was locked with a similar kind of alarmed laser field as the roof door. Even if my Medusa abilities hadn't been taken away from me, I'd have struggled to open it. And I could see straightaway that Jack's card wouldn't be any more use here than it had been upstairs.

'Oh my goodness, I'm so sorry.' Amy's bottom lip trembled and she sank to the floor. 'I can't believe it's all gone so wrong.'

'It's okay, we're here now.' Ed put his arm round her.

I squatted down on the floor in front of her. 'What happened, Amy?' I asked.

'Where's Avery?' Cal demanded.

'I was being Foster,' Amy said breathlessly. 'I'd just ordered them to turn off the camera at the checkpoint. I'd said that it wasn't working properly ... that there was some electrical fault and they looked like that was a bit weird but

205

they did what I ordered and then I was about to tell them to leave the room so Avery and I could work out where the labs were when Foster called. The *real* Foster. And the guard who spoke to him realised I was really me and Foster ordered him to spray me with Medutox and ... I changed back to me.'

'What about Avery?' Cal's face was deathly pale.

'They took him away. I don't know where. And I don't know where Dylan and Harry are either, but ... but as soon as Foster heard they were in the building, he sent someone off to spray Dylan too.'

I clutched my forehead. This was bad. This was *really* bad. Far from rescuing the hit squad children and destroying Foster's ability to make Medusix, we were now all prisoners ourselves.

'But ... you came to us disguised as Dylan,' Ed said, looking confused. 'Why did Foster order that?'

'I wouldn't tell him about the rest of you, but as soon as he knew I'd ordered the checkpoint camera to be switched off, he worked out you were coming. There's a camera on the roof which isn't normally used but Foster got them to check it and he could see you all up there, trying to get through the door. When my Medutox wore off, Foster insisted I came up to get you back. He said you'd get away if he just sent the guards and that Dylan and Harry and Avery would die if I tried to trick him.' Amy's eyes filled with tears. 'Did I do the right thing?'

'Of course you did,' Ed said reassuringly.

'I still don't see why Foster made you come disguised as Dylan?' Cal said with a frown.

'Because Foster said Jack had told him how protective you are of me. He thought if I came up as me then there'd be an argument over one of you taking me to safety. If you thought I was Dylan, you'd just follow her inside.' Amy hesitated. 'Basically I think he thinks you think that I'm a useless little kid and Dylan's, like, mega tough.'

I stood up and leaned against the wall, closing my eyes. This last detail was almost the worst thing we'd just been told. It showed how intimately Foster understood us – and the relationships between us.

There was a shuffling sound next to me. I opened my eyes. Amy was standing in front of me. Ed was watching her carefully but it was me Amy was looking up at, her eyes huge and round and full of emotion.

'You don't think I'm a useless little kid, do you, Nico?' she asked plaintively.

'No, of course he doesn't,' Ed said. 'You got Avery, Dylan and Harry *in* here, Amy.'

I looked at Amy's plump face, remembering how she'd stayed looking like Ketty so I would kiss her. If it hadn't been for that, Ketty and I would have been fine before she died whereas ... and this was the terrible truth I realised I had been refusing to face ... when Ketty died we were barely speaking.

And that was totally Amy's fault.

'Well, you're useless and a kid,' I said, looking her up and down with as scathing an expression as I could manage. 'Though you're certainly not "little".'

Amy gasped. Hurt filled her eyes. She stood up and walked across the room, her shoulders shaking.

Ed glared at me, his fists clenched at his sides. He called me a name I'd never heard him use before – then he stalked off to sit with Amy who was now weeping in the corner.

Cal raised an eyebrow. 'Nice work, bro,' he said sarcastically.

'Shut up,' I said. But inside I was already regretting what I'd said. Not just because I'd upset Amy and not just because we needed to be focusing on getting out of this room instead of arguing with each other – but because if Ketty had been here she would have told me I was being stupid and unkind.

And she would have been right.

'Okay.' I pushed myself off the wall I'd been leaning against. 'First thing we have to do is avoid being disabled with Medutox again.'

Ed stared at me. 'And how do you suggest we do that?' he said.

I gulped. Amy was still sobbing in the corner, her face covered with her hands.

'Well,' I said. 'Medutox works because you breathe it in, doesn't it?'

'So?' Cal said.

I glanced round the room. 'There's no vent here they can release it through. They weren't expecting to keep us locked up like this. I'm guessing they're going to have to spray us by hand.'

Ed shrugged. 'How does that help?'

'We have to cluster round the door when they come in and allow them to spray us. If we can keep the dose to a minimum and hold our breath then—'

'That's ridiculous,' Ed snorted. 'Medutox is a vapour. It travels through the air. We can't escape it.'

'Maybe not, but we can try,' I said. 'We hold our breath. We cover our faces. We move away from the door. Maybe we won't all manage not to breathe it in, but any one of us could get us out of here if we had our powers back. We've all got amazing abilities.' I looked over at Amy as I said this, but she still hadn't looked up.

'It's worth a try,' Cal said.

Ed shrugged again. 'Okay, but it's not going to work.'

'Amy?' I said. 'What do you think?'

Amy lifted her head. She wiped her eyes and faced me at last.

'Like Cal says,' she said with a sniff. 'It's worth a try.'

Twenty-five minutes later the guards were back. One stood in the door, braced ready for us to attack. The other stepped into the room. Immediately we got to our feet, standing quietly in a row. The man frowned; he clearly wasn't expecting us to be so docile. He lifted his can of Medutox and sprayed it at Amy. I held my breath as he moved the can across to Ed, then Cal. More quick sprays. Then it was my turn. I closed my eyes. The mist lit on my eyelids.

It was over. The guard left. I raced across to the far corner of the room, wiping my face and, finally, allowing myself a tiny breath through the fabric of my jacket. I stayed huddled over for several minutes, breathing as shallowly as possible.

Whether my plan could work depended on how long the Medutox stayed active once it was sprayed into the air ... if it was longer than a few seconds, then there was no way we could disable it. But – from the way our enemies had used it in the past, trying to trap us in confined spaces – I was guessing it didn't stay potent for long.

After about five minutes, I lifted my face. The others were already breathing normally, sitting against the back wall of the empty room.

I held out my hand, attempting to deploy my telekinesis to move Cal's jacket – which dangled from his hand. Nothing happened. I tried again. Still nothing.

I moved over to the door anyway. I could attempt to figure out the laser alarm system, even if I couldn't control it. As I stood there, my confidence faltered. I hadn't managed to unlock this kind of door up on the roof. What made me think I could manage it now?

I took a deep breath and tried to clear my mind. Images of Ketty kept pushing their way into my head. Ketty laughing at something funny I'd said ... Ketty all tough and determined, running around the grounds at Fox Academy ... Ketty frowning with concentration as she tied her hair with a piece of string ... Ketty coming back over the cliff top months ago, her eyes shining at me. *I knew you'd save me ... that's what I saw ... that's what had to happen ...*

I suddenly wondered if Ketty had foreseen her own death. If she had, she hadn't said anything ... but then I hadn't made it easy for her to talk to me. I'd been mean to her ... I hadn't listened ... I hadn't shown her how much she meant to me.

I'd pushed her away.

Tears suddenly pricked at my eyes. I stared at the locked door, its handle swimming in front of me. What was the point of escaping? What was the point of anything without her?

'Ketty knew that you loved her.' Amy's voice was a timid whisper beside me.

I glanced round at her. She was shuffling from foot to foot beside me. Ed and Cal were still sitting with their backs against the far wall, chatting in low voices.

'Excuse me?' My voice was hoarse. I felt broken, like I was in little pieces.

'Ketty knew you loved her. I mean, it was obvious to everyone,' Amy said. 'And I'm sorry I didn't change back straight away that ... that time ... I ... I ...' She tailed off, blushing a deep red. 'I just ... it was just hard to stop ...'

I looked at her, suddenly aware of how much it was costing her to make this confession to me.

'Thanks, Amy,' I stammered. 'I'm sorry I was mean earlier. I didn't ... it isn't true. You're cool.'

Amy's blush deepened and it struck me how young she

211

was – just Ed's little sister, caught up in a terrible situation that wouldn't be happening if we didn't have Medusa powers.

'I wish none of us had been given the Medusa gene,' I said.

Amy looked me in the eye. 'Well, we were,' she said, sounding for a moment just like Ketty. 'So we might as well make it work for us.' She indicated the door again. 'How's it going with the lock?'

'It's really difficult.' I could hear the shake in my voice as I spoke. 'I don't know if I can do it.'

'Of course you can,' Amy said.

Again, she sounded just like Ketty. The thought made me smile. Without thinking about it too hard, I turned towards the door and breathed out, directing all my energy to the lock, holding the visualisation more lightly than usual, but concentrating as deeply as I had ever done in my life.

With a soft groan, the door popped open. I stared at it, amazed. Beside me, Amy gasped. 'You did it.' I held out my hand and tried to lift the corner of Amy's jacket. Nothing happened. What on earth was going on?

Across the room, Cal and Ed scrambled to their feet. My heartbeat quickened. Was this some sort of trap? How had my telekinesis come back just for one moment, then gone again? Well, there was no time to worry about it now. I turned to the others. 'Come on,' I said.

'What do we do now?' Amy asked.

'Whatever it is, we need to stick together,' Ed urged.

'We have to find Avery, Dylan, Harry and the kids Foster conned into coming here,' Cal said.

'Yes,' I agreed. 'Then we can get to the lab and destroy it.' I peered into the corridor outside. It was empty. I crept through, the others behind me, and headed for the stairs.

We were on our way.

28: Timing is Everything

I led Cal, Ed and Amy along the corridor, still bewildered by how I'd managed to open the door. The upper floor of the complex was small – far smaller than at ground level. We passed a couple of offices, complete with desks and computers, but none of them were occupied. There was no sign of any CCTV cameras either, but I still kept looking anxiously round, wondering if anyone had seen us.

We stopped at the top of the stairs. I tried to visualise the ground-floor plan of the building, which Harry had hacked into earlier. There were two large rooms on either side of the front entrance, then about eight or nine smaller ones towards the back. Trouble was we had no idea what most of the rooms were used for.

'Comms, rescue and lab,' I muttered under my breath.

'What's that?' Ed whispered behind me.

'Our original plan,' I whispered back. 'Take out all the communications links so that the CCTV and the alarms stop working ... find the hit squad children – plus Harry,

Dylan and Avery – and get them to safety ... destroy Foster's lab.'

Ed nodded but he looked scared.

I was scared too. This was an overwhelming task and – despite the earlier miracle of the laser-alarmed door – none of us would properly be in possession of our Medusa skills for at least another twenty minutes.

I crept down the stairs, sweat beading on the back of my neck. Voices rose up from the ground floor. One man was talking to another. 'Foster's on his way,' he said.

Great. My heart – already in my guts – plummeted to my shoes. That was all we needed ... Foster himself. I stopped at the bend in the stairs and peered round and down. A long corridor stretched both ways at the bottom of the steps. Amy must know where the comms centre was – she'd been there earlier – but I had no idea which direction to take for the lab – and no sense of where the others might be imprisoned. Again, I felt Ketty's absence. If she were here, she might have been able to see into the future and find out. I forced the thought of her away and crept on ... down, down to the bottom step.

Without warning, all the lights went out and the corridor was plunged into darkness. I flattened myself against the wall. I could feel Ed's presence beside me, his breathing sharp and rapid.

'Oh my goodness, what's happening?' Amy hissed from his other side.

'Ssh,' I whispered. Someone ran past us. I could hear their

footsteps, though it was impossible to make out more than a shadowy outline in the pitch black.

I was still on the bottom step. As I felt for the ground below, a hand reached round the corner and grabbed my arm. I almost yelled out, but the hand squeezed my wrist.

'Nico, it's Avery.'

'Avery?' Relief washed over me. 'What happened? Are you okay?'

'I'm fine,' Avery whispered.

Ed, Cal and Amy were down the stairs now. We clustered around Avery.

'What's going on?' Cal hissed.

'There's no time,' Avery whispered. 'Follow me.'

He led us left along the corridor. More shouts echoed ahead of us as we reached a door.

'In here.' Avery opened the door and led me through. The others bustled in after us. We were in some kind of room with high tables and stools. I couldn't make out more detail in the dim light.

Avery crossed the room and took us through another door. As we herded inside, he shut the door and took out a small torch from his pocket. It illuminated his face from underneath, casting the lines of his nose and mouth into deep shadow. I glanced around. Cal, Ed and Amy looked similarly spooky in the torchlight. I shivered.

'Where are we?' I asked.

'How did you get free?' Amy added.

'What's happening with the lights?' Cal said.

'Do you know where Dylan and Harry are?' That was Ed.

Avery cleared his throat. 'Okay, slow down. One at a time.' He paused, clearly trying to collect his thoughts. 'They were holding me in their communications room,' he said. 'I could see some of the CCTV screens and you guys showed up a minute ago when you were at the top of the stairs. I distracted the guard watching the screens from noticing until you'd got past. Then the lights just suddenly went out and the screens went blank and the guard rushed off. I don't know what happened – and I don't think he did either.'

'Maybe it was a power cut,' Ed suggested.

'Perhaps,' Avery agreed.

I thought back to the way I'd managed to open the door upstairs earlier. Had that been due to a temporary power failure too? It seemed unlikely.

'Anyway the guard left me in what he obviously thought was a locked room – but the doors work on electronic alarms so it wasn't hard for me to get out. To be honest, as long as the whole complex is in darkness with all the security down, I'm guessing they won't even notice I'm gone.'

'So why did you bring us in here?' I said.

'Look,' Avery said. He shone the torch around the room. There were high tables in here, just as in the outer room. But also a sink and shelves containing bottles and jars and a row of microscopes and two computers, side by side.

'Oh my goodness,' Amy breathed.

'It's the lab,' Cal said.

'Exactly.' Avery swung the torch back so all our faces were illuminated. 'This is our chance to destroy all Foster's Medusix research, but we have to hurry, the guards will be back any second.'

'Excellent,' I said. 'Ed, what does this oil you said Foster uses to make Medusix look like?'

'Er . . .' Ed blinked rapidly. 'Back at the castle it came in barrels. They had a stamp on the front.'

'Okay, let's look,' I said. 'We can use the oil to blow up the lab. But hurry. It's not just the guards. The lights and alarm system could come back on at any moment.'

It was hard exploring the lab by the light of just one torch. We walked round the edges of the room, Avery shining the torch into every corner. It took about a minute to find the barrels of oil. They were propped against the far wall, under the only window in the room.

Ed immediately bent down and attempted to lift one of the barrels. It was clearly heavy as he could only just raise one edge off the ground.

'Good, they're full,' he said.

'Maximum impact,' I said. 'Roll a barrel into each corner.'

I took one myself. Avery took another, while Cal, Ed and Amy rolled a third. Seconds later, everything was in place.

'Okay, we're done,' Avery said.

I hesitated. 'What about Dylan and Harry?' I said. 'Because I'm guessing there's a lot of flammable stuff in here. The fire could easily spread.'

'Yeah,' Cal said, catching on fast. 'The whole building will probably go up.'

'Exactly,' I said. 'We need to make sure Harry and Dylan are safe – and those children Foster conned into his hit squad too.'

Avery's face fell. 'I heard the guards talking about them but I didn't see where they were. The CCTV from wherever they're being kept wasn't playing on any of the screens I saw.'

'Okay, this is what we should do,' I said.

The others looked at me expectantly.

'Avery stays here, ready to blow up the lab,' I said. 'Ed, Amy and I will go and find the others.'

'What about me?' Cal asked.

'You come with us as far as the communications centre in case there's a problem,' I said. 'Then you get back to Avery in the lab and barricade yourselves in.'

'I don't get it,' Cal protested. 'Why do I need to come back? It doesn't take two people to ignite the oil in the lab.'

'If anyone should stay behind,' Ed added, 'I'd rather it was Amy.'

'Listen,' I said. 'It has to be this way round. We need Amy with us to impersonate Foster. And Cal needs to get back here so he can get Avery out of the lab when they've ignited the oil.'

'Explain this, Nico,' Avery said with a frown.

'Okay, once we've reached the comms room, Ed, Amy and I will head off to find the others. When we're sure

219

they're safe, Ed will let Cal know telepathically. You two set light to the oil. Then Cal will fly you both out of the window before the whole place goes up.'

'But the window is locked,' Ed pointed out. 'And the Medutox means you can't unlock it, Cal can't fly out of it – and I can't communicate telepathically.'

I thought back. How long was it since we'd last been sprayed? Surely the effects of the Medutox would have eased up by now?

I raised my hand towards the window above the barrels of oil and gave my wrist a swift flick. The window sprang open.

'It's worn off,' I said with a grin. 'Go on, Ed, try contacting Dylan.'

Ed screwed up his face, focusing on making the remote connection.

'Okay, Nico.' Avery sounded reluctant. 'I don't like it, but I can't see another way.'

'We'll be fine,' I said. 'Amy, can you pretend to be Foster again?'

'Sure.' As she spoke, Amy began the transformation.

Ed sighed as he turned to me. 'I can't reach Dylan,' he said. 'I think she must still be under the Medutox. But I can reach everyone else.'

'Well, that's what matters right now.' I glanced at Amy. She now looked totally like Foster. My confidence surged. This was going to work.

'Come on,' I said. 'Let's go.'

29: Out of Time

We took the torch. Avery insisted that if we were negotiating the complex we would need it more than he did. I led the way out of the lab and into the dark corridor. In the distance I could hear men shouting. It surely wouldn't be long before someone either came to check on the lab – or reactivated the lights and alarm system.

'Which way to the comms room?' I whispered.

'Down there,' Amy said softly, pointing to the right.

As we crept along the corridor, I took a proper look at her. Apart from the scared expression on her face she looked identical to Foster. Except ... I looked down at her legs. She'd left the trousers of the man's suit she was wearing rolled up from when she'd been her own height earlier.

I gave her a nudge. 'You might want to rethink the turn-ups,' I whispered. 'Not very "bossman".'

'Oh my goodness ...' Amy hissed. Even in the dark of the corridor I could tell she was blushing.

'Oh no.' Ed was pointing along the corridor. Torchlight

flickered on the wall ahead. Someone was coming towards us.

Amy was still busy unfurling her trouser legs. I looked around. We could make a dash back to the lab, but it was unlikely we'd get there before whoever had that torch saw us. I had no idea if there were other rooms we could hide in ... we certainly hadn't passed any doors or stairs so far.

We couldn't go down or sideways. Which left only one option.

'Fly me and Ed up to the ceiling,' I whispered at Cal.

His mouth fell open. Then he grabbed our wrists. I just had time to shove the torch into Amy's hands before Cal zoomed upwards. Still clutching my wrist, he spun us in the air until we reached the fluorescent light strip that ran along the centre of the ceiling. Stretched out along its length we clung to the light, hooking our ankles over the far end. I had to use all my stomach muscles to stop the middle portion of my body sagging down. Ahead of me, on Cal's other side, Ed was clinging on for dear life too.

Beneath us, Amy was still standing, the torch in her hand. My heart thundered in my ears. Suppose the light fitting we were clinging to suddenly got switched on? Suppose Amy – pretending to be Foster down there on her own – couldn't handle the encounter she was about to have? Suppose whoever was coming happened to swing their torch upwards to where Cal, Ed and I were hiding on the ceiling?

Amy shook herself, then walked forward. The gentle glow from her torch surrounded her. Another of Foster's men was approaching. I could see him quite clearly now, thanks to the light from both his torch and Amy's.

'What are you doing here?' Amy barked.

She sounded convincingly like Foster.

'I was coming to check on the labs, sir,' the other man said.

I froze. Amy had to stop him from going there. Otherwise Avery would be discovered before we'd had a chance to find Harry and Dylan.

'*What?*' Amy spat out the word. I was pretty certain she was trying to think on her feet . . . buying herself a little time.

There was an awkward pause below. I held my breath.

'The labs, sir,' the man stammered. 'I . . . I thought some-one should check there hadn't been a breach of—'

'I've just come from the labs,' Amy as Foster barked. 'Everything's secure. You should be working on getting the lights and door locks working again. Not thinking for your-self coming down here.'

'Yes, sir.' The man bowed his head. He took a few steps away from Amy. 'Sorry, sir, I'll get back to the others.'

'Hurry!' Amy-as-Foster snapped.

The man turned and scurried off. As the light from his torch disappeared around the corner, Cal flew us carefully down to the ground.

Amy still looked like Foster, but she was breathing in fast, shallow gasps as we reached her.

'Oh my goodness,' she whispered. 'I'm shaking.'

'You were awesome, Amy,' I said with a grin. 'Really,

you saved us – and Avery back at the lab ... you saved everything.'

See, Ketty, I'm not so bad.

Ed stepped forward and gave his sister a hug. Amy beamed at us both.

A minute later and we reached the communications room. Cal left us, slipping silently back along the corridor towards Avery and the lab.

Ed and Amy looked at me expectantly. My plan had been to somehow draw one of the men outside and have Ed mind-read him to find out Dylan and Harry's location, but as I peered round the door, I realised this was going to be impossible. The room was brightly lit – thanks to a large lantern on one of the desks – and the three men it illuminated were all standing together, poring over a panel in the wall. One guy with a shock of red hair was applying a screwdriver to one of the circuit boards inside the panel. A second stood over him. The third, just behind and to the left, was the man that Amy, as Foster, had just sent back here.

'How much longer, Erik?' this third man asked. 'Foster's on the warpath. I just saw him. You gotta hurry.'

'I going fast as I can, Paul,' said Erik in broken English. He was still crouched over the wall panel. 'This sabotage for sure, not power cut.'

I stepped backwards, out of sight. As I did so, the strip light above our head flickered and came on. The door beside us hummed. Along the corridor the sound of locks clicking back into place echoed towards us.

'Done!' Erik stood up. 'I hope Foster seeing how fast that was.'

I poked Amy, still looking like Foster, in the ribs. 'You're up,' I said. 'Go and get rid of them.'

Amy nodded. I could see Ed was about to protest that we shouldn't be putting her in harm's way again, but before he could speak, I clutched his arm and dragged him away, down the corridor.

Amy as Foster drew herself up.

'What are you doing in here?' she barked.

I couldn't see them from where I stood, but I could just imagine the three men in the room jumping to attention.

'Was deliberate sabotage, sir,' Erik said. 'I mend main circuit. We have power, lights. All alarms back on.'

'Good,' said Amy-as-Foster. 'Well done. All three of you need to get up to the first floor. Report of a disturbance in one of the ... rooms. You need to investigate. Now.'

'Yes, sir.'

Ed and I flattened ourselves against the wall as the three men rushed out of the room. They headed away from us, towards the stairs, without a glance in our direction.

As soon as they'd disappeared, I followed Amy into the comms room.

'You did really great,' I said. 'Again.'

Amy grinned. 'Thanks, Nico.'

Ed rushed over to a bank of TV screens that stood against one wall. He pressed the 'on' buttons of each terminal.

The screens flickered into life as I went over. They

showed CCTV from a selection of rooms around the complex. One was trained on the lab interior where Avery and Cal were visible pacing up and down between the tables. I could just make out the edge of a table on its side – clearly part of the barricade they'd made to keep themselves secure inside the lab until we contacted them.

Another screen revealed the three men Amy-as-Foster had just sent away – they were racing up the stairs to the first floor.

My heart thudded. It wouldn't take them long to work out there was no one up there. Then they would be back to speak to their boss again.

The next two screens were empty. I glanced round the room. Surely there must be more CCTV than this? Another bank of screens across the room caught my eye. I rushed over and switched on the terminals.

Yes. More rooms and corridors around the building were revealed.

'Look,' Ed said, coming up behind me. He pointed to the screen at the end. It showed Harry surrounded by four kids, about ten or eleven years old. He was trying to push open a fire door. Dylan stood behind him, looking anxiously around. She held a tablet computer in her hand. As we watched, Harry turned to the tablet and examined the screen.

'It's them,' I said.

Amy rushed over.

It was obvious the fire door was locked. Harry was pushing at it again, but it wouldn't budge.

'Can't you do something to help them, Nico?' Ed asked.

'I'm too far away,' I said.

As I spoke, Harry consulted the tablet once more. He pressed down on the screen, then turned to the door again. This time it swung open.

We watched Harry usher the kids through. Dylan peered around her, then followed him.

'Come on,' I said. 'We need to get out ourselves.'

We raced out of the room and along the corridor. Footsteps sounded behind us. Clearly the men that Amy had sent upstairs were on their way back. We reached the fire door Harry and Dylan had just exited through. It was still unlocked. With a single twist of my hand, the door flew open ahead of us. We rushed out, into the cool night air. Across the hard, dark grass. Into the trees. I looked around. No sign of Harry, Dylan and the kids. They must have run into a different section of the trees.

'Can you reach Dylan yet?' I asked Ed as we stopped at last.

'No,' he said, panting for breath. 'She must still be under the Medutox.'

I peered out of the trees. *There.* Dylan and Harry were running towards us from another part of the woodland about twenty metres to the left. Dylan was in the lead, Harry, limping, was struggling to keep up. The four younger kids ran alongside him.

'Okay, Ed,' I said. 'They're safe. Give Avery and Cal the go-ahead.'

Ed gave me a swift nod, then turned away, focusing on the middle distance.

I stepped out of the trees and waved at Dylan. She waved back and shouted something.

What was she thinking, yelling out like that? I darted back under cover. Man, Dylan was going to attract serious attention making such a noise.

'Is it done, Ed?' Amy asked.

Ed nodded. 'Cal and Avery are setting light to the oil now. The explosion's going to happen any moment.'

I looked again at Dylan. She was really gaining on Harry now. I peered more closely at him. He was limping quite badly. Was he injured?

At last Dylan ran up. She was gasping for breath, holding up the tablet computer we'd seen earlier.

'Issketisheesalie,' she gabbled.

'What?' I said. 'Are you guys okay?'

Dylan nodded, her eyes glinting in the moonlight.

'Look,' she said. She pressed a button on the screen. It fizzled into life. A black and white image of a small room with a single bed came into view.

'What's that?' I said, looking away and across the grass towards the complex. The explosion should happen any second now.

'*Look*, Nico,' Dylan gasped again.

I looked at the tablet computer in time to see someone walk across the room, their back to the camera.

I stared at the screen, unable to believe what I was watching.

'It's Ketty,' Dylan said with a moan. 'She's alive.'

As she spoke, Ketty turned round. Her face – her beautiful face – filled the screen. A terrible confusion of emotions flooded through me – disbelief and hope . . . and terror.

'Where?' I grabbed Dylan's arm. 'Where is she?'

Dylan pointed back to the complex. 'In there,' she said. 'A room – a cell, really – close to the lab.'

I stared at Ed in horror. He'd just told Cal and Avery it was okay to blow up the lab.

'Stop them!' I ordered.

'It's too late.' Ed's words were drowned out by the explosion. It rocked the ground. I spun round, my focus on the complex. There, flying out of the lab window, were Avery and Cal.

But all I could see was the fireball that rose from the side of the building they had just left.

And all I knew was that Ketty was still inside.

30: Walk Through Fire

'NO!' The yell erupted out of me. Without thinking . . . without even knowing what I was doing, my legs were carrying me towards the burning building.

I raced through the trees, my breath searing my lungs. If Ketty was there, I had to find her. I had to get her out of the complex even though – and I could barely face the thought that pressed against the edges of my consciousness – she was unlikely to have survived that bomb blast.

Dylan ran up beside me as I reached the edge of the trees. Her face was pale in the moonlight, her dark red hair streaming out behind her.

'Wait, Nico,' she panted, grabbing hold of my arm. 'You can't just barge into a burning building.'

'I have to get Ketty,' I said. 'How did you know she was there? Why didn't you rescue her along with the little kids?'

'I'm trying to explain,' Dylan said. 'Ketty wasn't in the same stretch of rooms that me and Harry and the hit squad children were put in. Foster had her off in some special cell. I saw her on the CCTV when they took us in, but we couldn't work out exactly where she was until Harry found this.' She held up the tablet computer.

'So?' I tried to pull my arm away from Dylan's hand but she gripped me more tightly. 'You said her cell was next to the lab. If you found her, why didn't you get her out?'

'I didn't say "next" to, I said "close" to,' Dylan said furiously. 'Ketty's cell is *underneath* the lab. It's in the basement. There's a row of tiny rooms where Foster keeps all his supplies. Ketty's in one of those. They're on a separate security loop to the rest of the building, so the power cut didn't open her door.'

'Did you actually go down there?' I asked.

'Yes, but the room was still locked. All that happened was that Harry got hurt.' She hesitated. 'I think Ketty's cell opens with that card Jack gave us.'

I stared at her, taking in what she was saying at last. I felt in my pocket. The card was still there.

'If she's in a basement room she might have been protected from the blast,' Ed said. He and Amy had appeared beside us. I'd been so intent on what Dylan was saying I hadn't even noticed. I glanced up. Cal and Avery were clear of the building now. They were heading for the spot where Harry was waiting with the little kids. Neither of them had noticed us.

'But she won't be protected from the smoke,' Dylan added. 'They're getting the Medutox into her through the air

231

vents which means she doesn't have long before the fumes get to her.'

'So why are we waiting?' I shook off Dylan's arm at last. 'I have to get inside.'

'You won't get past the fire,' Dylan argued. 'That's why you have to wait.' She checked her watch. 'My Medutox should wear off in another couple of minutes ... then I'll get us both in ...'

'I'm coming too,' Ed said. 'If we meet someone on the way, I can hypnotise them.'

I gazed at them. Part of me wanted to tell them to stay behind, but – if I was honest – I knew I might well need their help. 'I don't—'

'She's my friend too,' Ed insisted. 'Foster managed to make me think she was dead before.'

A lump rose in my throat at the desperate look on his face. 'Have you tried to contact her remotely?' I asked him.

'Yes, but I'm not getting anywhere,' he said.

'That's because she's being given Medutox,' Dylan said. 'Like we were.'

'Okay, you can both come.' My voice sounded gruff, like it didn't matter much either way. But I knew I wasn't fooling either of them.

'What about me?' Amy said.

'No.' Dylan and Ed spoke together. 'I can move faster if I'm only protecting two people,' Dylan added.

'You should go and find Cal and Avery,' I said. 'Let them know what's happening.'

Amy nodded.

Dylan checked the time again. 'Not long now till the Medutox wears off.'

I looked over at the complex. Men were pouring out of the building now. Smoke billowed upwards out of shoots of fire. The walls were barely visible under the licking flames. You could feel the heat from here. Shouts and yells filled the air.

Seconds passed. I fidgeted impatiently.

'Okay,' Dylan said. 'My power is back.'

'Come *on*!' I set off across the grass again, out of the cover of the trees. If any of the men spilling out of the building had looked over they would have seen us, but all eyes were on the front of the complex, where the fire raged hardest.

I led us round to the back of the building. Here the flames were smaller and the smoke not quite so dense. I stopped running. Dylan and Ed raced up.

'Get behind me,' Dylan ordered.

Ed and I stood on either side of her so that we formed a triangle. I realised my hands were trembling. I reached up and focused on the door straight ahead of us. I gave my wrist a sharp twist. The door swung open. Smoke poured out. I felt Dylan's force field surge around me. It would protect us from the fire, I knew, but we still needed oxygen.

'I can get us to Ketty's cell in about a minute,' Dylan said. 'But remember the smoke will get through like Medutox does, so you'll have to hold your breath until we're past it. Okay?'

Ed and I nodded. I took a deep breath.

Dylan set off. Ed and I stayed close behind her. Into the building. Smoke swirled around us. The heat was intense. Dylan walked us through the flames. Every now and then her force field weakened, especially under my feet, and I felt the scorching fire creep closer. It was terrifying to be so close to the flames, to see and hear their raging crackle and hiss.

The pressure in my lungs was building as Dylan led us along the corridor. The smoke darkened as we walked. For a moment it was impossible to see the walls on either side, then the smoke cleared – enough to reveal a door on the left. Dylan carefully took hold of the handle and opened it. A short flight of stairs appeared before us. We raced down. The fire and smoke were lighter here. Through another door. The air suddenly cooled around us.

There were no flames. No acrid fumes here. I looked up. No sign of damage to the ceiling – on the other side of which the lab explosion had occurred.

I felt Dylan release the force field. I breathed in deeply. My heart beat faster. If Ketty was down here, the chances were good that she'd survived the initial blast.

'How did you find her?' I asked as we raced along.

'Harry did it,' Dylan said. 'He hacked into the security system and found out how to release our rooms and the door to the one you were in.'

So *that* was how it had opened – nothing to do with my telekinetic skills after all.

'Anyway,' Dylan went on breathlessly. 'We found Ketty but Harry couldn't see how to release her door. The power cut didn't help either.'

'Harry caused that power cut?' Ed asked admiringly.

'Yeah, we hoped it might open Ketty's cell door as well as the labs, but it didn't,' Dylan said.

We reached a crossroads. 'Along here,' Dylan said, speeding down the right-hand corridor.

I ran up beside her. 'Did Ketty see you before?' I asked. 'Does she know we're here?'

'No,' Dylan said. 'There was no way of contacting her. I saw her through a glass panel, but she couldn't see me.'

I opened my mouth to ask her what she meant, but a second later it was obvious. Dylan stopped outside a large metal door. A small window was set into the door at eye level. I peered through. There was Ketty. She was pacing up and down the room, her forehead furrowed with a frown. My stomach seemed to fall away inside me as I saw her. She was *here*. Just on the other side of this door.

I banged on the metal. 'Ketty!' I yelled. 'Ketts!'

'It's no good,' Dylan said. 'I tried all that. The room's obviously soundproofed. And that glass panel in the door is one way, so she can't see us.'

I peered inside again. Ketty was now sitting on the edge of the tiny camp bed that lined one wall. The room couldn't be more than two metres square. A metal box. I kept staring in at her, willing her to look up. Which was crazy, of course, as she wouldn't have been able to see me, even if she had.

'Nico, where's the card Jack gave us?' Ed said impatiently.

'Hurry!' Dylan added. 'The fire *will* spread here. And Foster's men are still outside.'

I pulled out the card. My fingers fumbled and it fell to the floor. Ed picked it up and gave it to me. My hand trembled as I held it over the swipe strip by the door. My nerves were jumping all over the place. I couldn't focus ... couldn't even breathe ...

'Nico, get a grip!' Dylan snapped beside me.

I took a deep breath and swiped the card. The door gave a *pop* as it opened. Ketty's head shot up, those golden-brown eyes fixed on the door.

Suddenly I couldn't move. My legs felt like lead. Impatient beside me, Dylan pushed at the door. I took a step forward. Almost stumbled. Looked up.

She was here, flying into my arms.

I held her tight, my cheek against the top of her head, my heart pumping so hard it felt like it would burst. Neither of us spoke but I knew that, however long I lived and however great my life became, no moment would ever feel better than this one.

It felt like no time passed, then I became aware of Dylan shouting in my ear.

'Nico, will you *come on*!'

Ketty and I pulled away from each other. I was aware of Dylan and Ed beside us. Ketty was looking around, smiling at them, but I couldn't tear my eyes away from her.

'I knew you would come,' she said, looking back at me, her fingers fluttering over the dark bruise on my cheek. 'I saw in a vision back in the castle, after they saved me from the water. I was semi-conscious for ages then they brought me here. My leg was just bruised, so I'm fine and . . .'

'Guys, we really need to go,' Ed said.

I shook myself. He was right. We still faced a huge challenge to escape the building. It was going to take all Dylan's powers to protect the three of us – and the fire upstairs would be raging harder than ever.

I grabbed Ketty's hand. 'Come on.'

We rushed back to the stairs we'd come down earlier. As we got closer, the ceiling above us gave a warning creak. I looked up. Cracks were splintering across the white plaster which was flaking down. Swirls of smoke were drifting through too.

The whole thing was about to collapse.

'We can get through!' Dylan shouted.

'No!' Ed grabbed her arm.

'Get back!' I shouted.

The ceiling gave a huge crack. I dragged Ketty backwards. Ed and Dylan stumbled after us. Another crack. More plaster.

And then the whole ceiling caved in.

31: The Way Out

My lungs filled with plaster dust. I bent over, coughing.

'No!' Ketty wailed.

I straightened up. The whole ceiling – from just beyond where we were standing to the stairs – had collapsed. Piles of rubble blocked our exit.

'Now what?' Ed clutched at his forehead. Like the rest of us he was covered in dust – and choking.

It wasn't just the dust. Smoke from the room above was now whirling overhead. The fire had found its way down to us at last.

'Along here!' I turned and pounded along the corridor. Surely there had to be another way out?

I ran, pulling Ketty behind me. The smoke and dust eased slightly. Ketty's slim wrist was real in my hand. She was alive. I still couldn't believe it. I wanted nothing more than to stop and hold her again. But we had to find a way out of the building before the rest of the ceiling collapsed and the fire engulfed us.

Around a corner. Along another corridor. Stairs leading up to the ground floor appeared at the end. I speeded up.

'No, Nico!' Ed yelled after me. 'They lead up to the centre of the building. We'd never get through the fire there.'

I skidded to a halt. Ketty stopped, breathless, beside me. I turned to Dylan.

'Can't you protect us all?' I said.

She shook her head. 'I could maybe look after myself. But extending the energy round three of you ... where the fire's at its worst ... there's no way ...'

My stomach screwed into a knot. I slid my hand fully into Ketty's and gripped it tightly. The others all looked at me expectantly.

'We'll find a way,' I said. I looked back along the corridor we'd just run down. There were two rooms on either side.

'Let's check these out,' I said. 'See if there's a window we could open.' It was a long shot. Ketty's cell hadn't had windows and nothing I'd seen in the rest of the basement so far suggested there were any elsewhere down here. But it was all I could think of.

Smoke was already curling around the corner we'd just run round.

'Move!' I said.

Dylan and Ed raced into the rooms on the right. Ketty and I ran through the first door on the left. Some kind of storage area full of cardboard boxes. No windows.

I looked around, suddenly feeling helpless. We were trapped down here.

Ketty reached up and touched my face again. Her fingers were cool on my cheek.

'I'm sorry I was so angry with you about ... about Amy pretending to be me ... it wasn't your fault. It wasn't even really hers, she's just a kid.'

I gazed into her golden-brown eyes. 'Maybe it was a bit my fault,' I said. 'I mean, I did act like an idiot, going off on my own and ... and ...' I took a deep breath, '... showing off and stuff ...'

Ketty smiled.

'When I thought you were ... gone ...' I said, struggling for the words, '... I realised that nothing else mattered except you not ... being gone ...'

'Me too,' she said.

We stared at each other for another second, then Ketty shook herself.

'Where are the others? D'you think they found something?' she said.

Taking her hand again, we re-entered the corridor. It was rapidly filling with smoke now. We didn't have much time. We crossed over to the door I'd seen Dylan fly through just seconds before.

Unlike the other rooms, this one was in darkness. I stood in the doorway, trying to adjust to the shadowy interior. Beside me, Ketty gasped. She pointed across the floor to where Dylan lay sprawled. She was moaning, clutching her head. A figure was bending over her. As we watched, open-mouthed, he stood up.

It was Foster.

'How dare you do this to me?' He glared at us. 'How dare you destroy my work?'

I was so shocked that, for a second, I thought it was Amy again, impersonating Foster. But the look of furious contempt in his eye was utterly genuine. I glanced at Ketty. She looked terrified. Anger rose up in me.

'How dare *you* kidnap Ketty and con those children into forming your own personal team of assassins?' I snapped. 'The Medusix you've created doesn't even work properly yet. You're using those kids like lab rats. Your own nephew collapsed after—'

'Nico.' Ketty gripped my hand more tightly, warning me not to provoke Foster further.

Foster let out an impatient snarl. 'That's what this lab was for ... developing the drug so it *would* work. And now you've destroyed it. Everything's gone.'

'Everything?' I could hear the hope in Ketty's voice.

My own spirits soared. If the lab was gone, then our mission had succeeded.

'Everything,' Foster repeated. 'All the samples ... the formulae ... the research notes ... it's all destroyed.' He paused. '*I'm* destroyed.'

I stared at him. Dylan was still prostrate at his feet, eyes closed, emitting low moans. But Foster was making no effort to stop us from running away. He might have hit Dylan, but he hadn't pulled a gun on us. And then I realised that he had no need to do any of these things. He knew the fire would get us. The fire would get all of us.

241

'Is that why you came down here?' I said. 'To go down with your ship?'

'I saw you coming towards the complex. I couldn't see how many of you, but I knew you were coming for Ketty,' Foster said. 'And I wanted to be here too. To make sure.'

'Sure of what?'

'That if I'm not going to survive this, then you aren't either.'

Nico? Ed's voice sounded in my head. *I'm next door. Does Foster have a gun?*

Probably, though he hasn't drawn it. But he's more or less knocked Dylan out. She's on the ground.

I've found a way out. I just need a minute.

I glanced up and down the corridor. I couldn't see either end of it, the smoke was now so thick. Its acrid scent was creeping towards us. Ketty coughed.

Hurry up! I thought-spoke.

'Contemplating your own mortality, Nico?' Foster asked nastily. 'Or working on your exit strategy?'

Keep him talking, Ed thought-spoke. *Don't let him know I'm down here too.*

My mind whirled. I couldn't think of a single thing to say. Panic filled me. There was so little time and, somehow, Ketty and I had to get a barely conscious Dylan away from Foster *and* stop him from following us into the next room.

Ask him about StopMed, Ed suggested.

'What's StopMed?' I said immediately.

Foster blinked, clearly shocked that I knew the name.

242

'How do you know about that?' he said.

I coughed. A wave of dark, acrid smoke swirled around us. I reckoned we had less than a minute before we started passing out.

'Is it another drug?' Ketty asked.

'It's designed to arrest the Medusa gene. Permanently,' Foster snapped. 'It was a by-product of the Medusix tests ... Obviously it hasn't been tested on live subjects.'

Okay, Ed's voice appeared in my head again. *It's time.*

There was no time to think. No time to hesitate. The smoke was in my eyes and up my nose and down my throat.

I raised my hands. Using all the focus I could muster, I twisted one wrist, raising Foster off his feet and flinging him against the wall. With the other, I lifted Dylan off the ground.

Still groaning with pain, she zoomed towards me. I guided her through the door. Ketty was already out, in the corridor. As she raced next door, I slammed the door shut. I raised Dylan again. Ran after Ketty. The room next door was bigger, full of stacked tables and chairs. No windows that I could see ... so where was this way out?

'Over here, Nico.'

I looked to the corner of the room. Ketty and Ed were bent down over an air vent. Ed had pulled the covering off, revealing a metre-square hole in the wall.

'It goes a couple of metres up,' he said. 'There's a ground-floor vent to the outside at the top. Can you get it open?'

I laid Dylan down, rushed over and peered up. The air

243

vent leading to the ground floor above our heads was clearly visible. A twist of my hand and the latch gave. Now we could get out.

'Done,' I said.

'Okay,' Ed said. 'Teleport me up there and outside. I'll help everyone else.'

Seconds later Ed was through the air vent. I looked round for Ketty.

'Dylan first,' she said.

Obediently, I teleported Dylan up off the floor and up through the vent. I waited till Ed had hold of her, then turned to Ketty.

'Your turn,' I said.

She leaned forward and kissed me. 'I'll be waiting up there,' she said.

I smiled and teleported her up.

Then I crawled into the vent myself. I stood up. My fingertips just reached the bottom of the opening to the ground floor. Ed's head and shoulders appeared above me. His face was barely visible, ghostly pale in the gloom. He reached out his hand. I grabbed his arm and braced myself. My ability to teleport only worked on others, not myself. I was going to have to use the wall as leverage to raise myself up a bit. Ed wouldn't be able to carry my weight alone, even if I moved him using telekinesis while he held on to me.

As I positioned my back and feet against opposite sides of the shaft, a bang echoed from next door. Was that Foster coming after us?

'Hurry up,' I gasped.

Ed strained, pulling on my arm. I inched up the shaft a few centimetres.

And then a hand clutched at my ankle.

'Get back here,' Foster roared.

I lost my grip on Ed – and my footing. I tumbled to the floor in a heap. Foster pulled me out. I tried to resist but I was weak from the smoke. It was thick in the room now, choking me.

Still holding me with one hand, Foster drew his gun.

'Only one bullet left,' he panted. 'I was saving it for myself, but now . . .' He pointed the gun at my head.

I stared in disbelief at the tiny metal barrel.

Was I going to die?

The smoke was filling my lungs. I didn't have much time either way. And then I looked into Foster's mean grey eyes and I thought of all the terrible things he had done and all the terrible things that had happened since I realised I had the Medusa gene and I knew that it couldn't end like this.

I couldn't let it.

Using all the power I had left. I turned the gun telekinetically, just as Foster pulled the trigger. The gun fired into the wall.

Foster stared at me. He let out a roar.

'Come on.' I stood a step towards the vent. 'We can both get out.'

'No,' Foster said bitterly. He backed away from me. 'No, I'm not—'

I felt fingers grab my shoulder from behind. With a *whoosh*, my body was sucked into the air ... I closed my eyes and sailed up, through a narrow space and into clear, fresh, beautiful air. I soared through space, eyes still tight shut, then landed with a thump on my back.

What had happened? I lay still, my head spinning, winded. And then I opened my eyes, just as Ketty fell on her knees beside me.

'Nico,' she breathed, her tears falling onto my cheek.

Was she real? I closed my eyes again, feeling hands under me ... lifting me ... carrying me away.

A minute or so later I was carried inside something – a car – and laid across a seat.

'Careful with his head,' someone said. Was that Fergus?

Voices were chattering around me. Doors slamming. An engine roared. Light danced across my closed eyelids.

I looked up.

My head was in Ketty's lap. She was smiling down at me.

'Am I alive?' I said.

'Yes.' That was Fergus.

I moved my head. Just a fraction. He was peering over his shoulder from the driver's seat at the front of one of the big cars we'd arrived in. Cal sat beside him.

'You did it,' Fergus said. 'You got Ketty and all the hit squad children are free. They're in the other car with Harry and Amy and Avery.'

'What happened to Foster?' Cal asked.

I gulped. The past few minutes already felt like a dream.

'I told him we could both get out,' I stammered, 'but he was too angry ...'

I closed my eyes. Foster must be dead by now.

'He got what he deserved,' Cal said angrily.

I looked up at Ketty. 'I tried to save him.'

She nodded. 'I know.

'What about Ed and Dylan?' I said, struggling to sit up.

'We're right behind you,' came Dylan's familiar drawl.

I looked over my shoulder. Ed and Dylan were sitting side by side. Dylan was holding the side of her head, but otherwise she looked fine.

'I hear you saved my life,' Dylan said.

I grinned. 'You can thank me later.' I stopped. 'But who saved mine?'

'That was Cal,' Ketty explained. 'When Ed saw Foster drag you back, he reached Cal remotely and Cal flew back and got you out.'

I gazed over at Cal. He smiled modestly.

'You see, Nico?' Ketty said, leaning over me again so that her dark curls brushed my face. 'We all did it ... together.'

32: StopMed

Avery and Fergus drove us to a hotel where we were able, at last, to rest. They called in a doctor to check us over as well. I know they would rather have taken us to hospital, but they were worried that if the UK government became aware of where we were, we would be taken away.

'They'll work it out eventually anyway,' Fergus had said with a sigh. He was right, of course. Less than a week ago, the government had planned to take us all back to Britain and put us under the protection of another agent to replace Geri Paterson. Their plans hadn't changed. The government still wanted us to continue as the Medusa Project, sending us on missions of their choosing to act out their agenda.

'Maybe we should just do what they want,' Ketty said. 'At least that means we stay as a group.'

The six of us – Ketty, me, Dylan, Ed, Cal and Amy – were in one of the hotel suites. Ed and Amy sat side by side on the edge of one of the beds. Dylan was sprawled across the other. Cal and Ketty were perched opposite them, on a large sofa. I paced up and down, past the window overlooking whatever rainy grey town we were in. The curtain material matched the cover on the bed and the cushions on the couch. The whole place was kind of depressing.

'Working for the UK government isn't much better than being in Foster's hit squad,' Dylan protested.

'I know,' Ed agreed. 'Even if we push the agent in charge of us to let us choose our own missions, they're still defining us by what we can do rather than by who we are.'

'Sorry, mate?' Cal said with a frown. 'You lost me there.'

I stopped pacing and turned around.

'What Ed means is that if we turn ourselves over to the government, or if they find us, then we'll be under their thumb forever,' I said.

'But what's the alternative?' Ketty sat up straighter on the sofa. She'd tied her hair back but two curls had escaped down either side of her face. They gave her features a soft, innocent appearance – but when I looked in her eyes I could see the pain and anxiety there. It was there in all of us now . . . a legacy of who we had become, thanks to the Medusa gene and the way our lives had been twisted because of it.

'The alternative is going into hiding, like Avery and Fergus planned for us back in Australia,' Dylan said glumly.

I nodded. Avery had already mentioned this option to me earlier. Basically, the plan was to split us up and send us to new locations around the world. This would mean us – and, in some cases, our families – taking on new identities and moving to different countries.

'But that's running away,' Cal protested.

'What do you think, Amy?' Ketty asked.

Amy looked up at her shyly. Since Ketty and I had been reunited, I'd noticed Ketty making a huge effort to be friendly to Amy ... almost as if she were trying to show me that she'd meant what she'd said. That all the upset over Amy pretending to be her was in the past. That too much was already stacked against us for anything to come between us.

'I wish we could just go back to England and go home and then go to Mr Fox's new school together when it opens in September,' Amy said.

Ketty and I exchanged looks. We'd already talked about how great it would be if this could happen. After our actions caused the destruction of Fergus's original school, Fox Academy, we'd been travelling around, living out of suitcases, for what felt like an eternity.

It was funny. There'd been many times when I was growing up in my stepfather's school, before I knew I had the Medusa gene, when I'd wished for a more exciting life. Now the idea of school and friends and living with Fergus again – with regular visits to Avery too – seemed like an impossible dream.

'If we go to Fergus's school then the government will find us in minutes,' Dylan said.

'Or else a bunch more criminals will try and use us like Foster did,' Cal added.

'So it's either let the government control us as the Medusa

Project,' Ketty said sadly, 'or live in hiding, apart from each other, always looking over our shoulders in case some bad guy tracks us down.'

Silence fell over the room. I turned and paced up and down again.

'Our options suck,' Dylan said, to no one in particular.

The others nodded.

'It's all because of our powers,' I said, sitting down on the sofa next to Ketty. I slid my arm across her shoulder. I couldn't bear the thought of being away from her. But I also didn't want to go on any more missions ... I didn't want to be used by anyone because I could move things with my mind. I didn't want to have to make spur of the moment decisions that ended with people dying. 'If we didn't have our Medusa abilities, we wouldn't be in this situation.'

'At least we destroyed the lab with the formula for Medusix.' Ketty reached across, leaning into me. 'At least nobody else is going to suffer.'

I knew she was thinking of Bradley, Foster's nephew. We'd had word – via Avery who'd made anonymous calls to both the politician on whom Foster had planted false information and the hospital where Bradley was being held – that the boy was conscious now, but that all his Medusa gifts had disappeared. Bradley would soon be on his way home to his mother. Without the powers he had temporarily possessed, he was just an ordinary kid.

'I wish we could be ordinary again.' I hadn't meant to

speak out loud. For a moment I tensed, expecting the others to protest. Well, maybe not Ed or Ketty – they'd never been wild about their abilities – and I wasn't sure about Amy, but I knew Cal loved his flying and Dylan had always enjoyed her Medusa gift too.

But to my surprise, all five of them just nodded.

And then Ed cleared his throat.

'There's a way we could be ordinary again,' he said. 'There's even a way we could go to Mr Fox's new school, all of us if we wanted. We could stay together. Live normal lives.'

'What are you talking about, Chino Boy?' Dylan raised her eyebrows. 'What about all the people trying to use us because of our powers?'

'I'm saying there's a way *not* to have our powers,' Ed said.

'StopMed,' I said, suddenly realising what Ed was referring to.

'What?' Cal asked.

'It came to me earlier when I was asking Avery to return that wallet and the lighter I stole after I stopped the train crash,' Ed said eagerly. 'It belonged to a student. He had a student card. ID. It meant I knew who he was . . . it made it easy to find him.'

'How is that relevant to us?' Dylan said impatiently.

'I knew that I wanted his life. An open, ordinary life.' Ed hesitated. 'And Foster has . . . had a drug that could give that life to us.'

The others all stared at him. I stood up.

'Ed's right,' I said. 'The drug is called StopMed.'

'Yes, Foster told us about it . . .' Ketty added. 'He said it was a by-product of developing Medusix and . . . and that it would counteract the effects of our Medusa gene.'

'But we blew up the lab,' Cal said. 'Even if the drug really exists, it would have been destroyed in the explosion.'

This was true. I shook my head. For a second, I'd thought there was a way out for us, but we were as trapped as ever.

'Er . . . actually not all the StopMed was destroyed.' Ed drew a slim sachet of pink powder from his pocket. He held it up. 'I found this back in the castle lab, before they moved everything to the complex.'

I stared at the powder. It was clearly labelled: *StopMed*. The dosage instructions were written underneath.

Ed looked around the room. 'I have to point out that Foster never tested the drug on humans with Medusa powers. He and his scientists only knew what it would do in theory, not practice.'

'It's worth the risk,' I said. 'We've got instructions on how to take it here. Does anyone else want this?'

'Yes.' All five voices spoke at once.

'Are you all sure?' I asked. 'According to Foster, if we take StopMed, the effects will be permanent.'

'Good,' Ketty said. 'I don't want to know what's going to happen to me.'

'And I can live without prying into people's minds,' Ed added.

'What about you?' I asked Cal.

He shook his head. 'A week ago I'd have said no way. But now ... now I've seen people die, or thought I did ...' He looked over at Ketty. I hadn't witnessed their reunion, but I could only imagine how happy Cal must feel that the girl he hadn't been able to save had lived after all. To my surprise I wasn't jealous at all. Okay, so Cal thought Ketty was cool. Who wouldn't?

But Ketty had chosen me. That was all that mattered.

'I agree with Cal,' Amy added.

Everyone looked at Dylan. 'Who needs a Medusa ability?' She grinned. 'I can look after myself without a force field. Anyway, Harry doesn't have one and he's pretty cool.'

'We've all got lots of abilities,' Ed said thoughtfully. 'We're smart.'

'And strong,' Cal added.

'And resourceful,' Ketty said.

'Let's do it, then,' I said.

Cal and Ketty fetched some glasses from the sideboard in the suite and Ed spooned a teaspoon of powder into each one.

'It's three parts water to one part powder,' he said.

Amy fetched a jug of water. Ed added the required amount and I handed round the glasses.

'Everyone ready?' I said.

The others nodded. Six hands rose to six mouths.

I gulped. Who would I be if I gave up my telekinesis? And then I looked at Ketty and my friends and smiled. There was only one way to find out.

254

'Cheers!' I said.

The glasses were drained in seconds. I could feel the liquid slipping down my throat. It had a cool, strangely chalky quality.

'How long does it take to work?' Amy asked nervously.

'I don't know,' Ed admitted. 'Anyone feel anything?'

'Give it a moment,' I said.

A long, silent minute ticked past. Nothing happened. We waited.

And waited.

And then, quite suddenly, I felt a cool wave of energy wash through my body. From the top of my head to the tips of my toes, it threaded gently through me and, like a ghost, it left, taking some intangible part of me with it.

I raised my hand slightly and focused on the cushion on the sofa beside Ketty. I willed it to rise into the air, but the power to make it happen wasn't inside me any more. The cushion stayed firmly on the couch.

'It's gone,' I said flatly.

'My force field's disappeared too,' Dylan said.

'And I can't fly.' That was Cal.

I looked at Ketty. 'I can't see into the future,' she said.

'Are you sure?' Dylan drawled. 'That ability of yours is real flaky.'

'Don't start, Dylan,' I said.

But Ketty just smiled. 'I'm sure,' she said.

'Oh my goodness, I can't change my face or my body,' Amy gabbled.

'Ed?' I said.

He nodded. 'I can't reach any of you remotely.' He looked me in the eyes. Instinctively I braced myself, ready for him to leap inside my mind. But nothing happened. 'Nope,' he said. 'It's all gone.'

We waited two hours, to make sure the effects of the StopMed weren't going to wear off, then we told Fergus and Avery what we'd done.

The relief on their faces was unmistakable, though they scolded us for taking the StopMed without letting them get it tested properly first. Still, as Ed pointed out, tests on a substance that conventional science doesn't understand wouldn't have helped much.

And that was how the Medusa Project ended.

All the stuff I've just told you about happened months ago. Fergus told the government we'd taken the StopMed. They interviewed us individually, realised we weren't bluffing, and let us go. By now we're sure the word will have got round to anyone who, like Foster, might be thinking of making use of us.

As far as we can be, we're safe. Right now we're at Fergus's new school – Foxrise Academy – waiting for tomorrow and the start of a new term and a new year.

Cal isn't here. He went back to Australia with Avery two days ago. I'm going out to visit them in the holidays. Everyone else took a vacation with their families but they're back now, ready for class. Fergus has done well, enrolling additional students as well as keeping most of the former ones, and we're expecting a lot of new faces tomorrow, plus all our old friends.

Amy's here too – she begged her parents to let her follow Ed to the school and, after much discussion, they agreed. I'm pleased. I like Amy – and Ed seems to come out of himself more when she's around too. Dylan still keeps herself to herself as much as possible. When everyone else went to stay with their families, she visited Harry and his mum, Laura. Harry got hurt during our escape, but he's okay now and the two of them are totally loved-up. Harry's smart – and tough. I don't think there are many people who could handle someone as difficult as Dylan, but he deals with her really well. It's fun teasing Dylan about it but, seriously, I'm glad she's got someone.

Ketty and I spend a lot of time together – she's back to her running. She's out in the grounds every morning – the fields and wood here aren't as big as at the old school, but Ketty says she prefers it.

If she's happy, I'm happy. It's funny thinking how I was just one year ago, when I first found out I had the Medusa gene. So much has happened since. Sometimes I feel like a different person from the one I was then. I'm certainly more thoughtful. More careful.

Every now and then I go out into the wood to meet Ketty after her run. I stand in a spot that reminds me of that moment twelve months ago when I tried to show her my telekinesis by making a stick on the ground travel telekinetically.

I usually try and move a twig or two. Old habits die hard, as they say.

But, just like back then, nothing ever happens.

If I'm honest, I kind of miss how special having the power of telekinesis made me feel. Then I remember how hard life was before.

I mean, I like things the way they are. I don't want the stick on the ground to twitch. And yet, part of me can't help wondering.

What would happen if it did?

SOPHIE McKENZIE

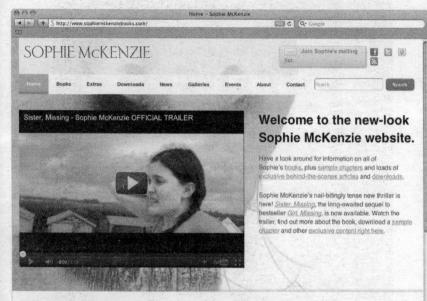

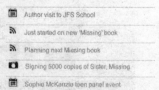

SOPHIE McKENZIE

SOPHIE McKENZIE

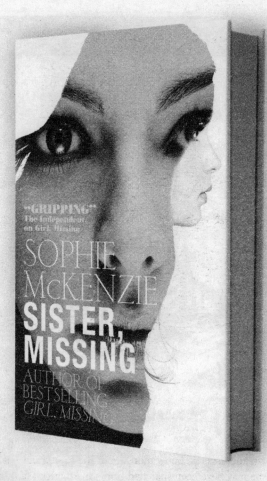

It's two years after the events of *Girl, Missing* and life is not getting any easier for sixteen-year-old Lauren, as exam pressure and a recent family tragedy take their toll. Lauren's birth mother takes Lauren and her two sisters on holiday in the hope that some time together will help, but a few days into the holiday one of the sisters disappears, under circumstances very similar to those in which Lauren was taken years before. Can Lauren save her sister, and stop the nightmare happening all over again?

ISBN 978-0-85707-288-7 (HB)
ISBN 978-0-85707-290-0 (eBook)

SOPHIE McKENZIE

RICHARD AND JUDY'S CHILDREN'S BOOKS WINNER 12+
WINNER OF THE RED HOUSE BOOK AWARD OLDER CATEGORY
WINNER OF THE BOLTON BOOK AWARD
WINNER OF THE MANCHESTER BOOK AWARD

Lauren is adopted and eager to know more about her mysterious past. But when she discovers she may have been snatched from an American family as a baby, her life suddenly feels like a sham. Why will no one answer her questions?
How can she find her biological mum and dad?
And are her adoptive parents really responsible for kidnapping her?

Lauren runs away from her family to find out the truth but her journey takes her into more and more danger – as she discovers that the people who abducted her are prepared to do anything to keep her silent.

ISBN 978-0-85707-413-3 (PB)
ISBN 978-1-84738-897-1 (eBook)

ABOUT THE AUTHOR

SOPHIE MCKENZIE was born and brought up in London, where she still lives with her teenage son. She has worked as a journalist and a magazine editor, and now writes full time. Her debut was the multi-award winning *Girl, Missing* (2006), which won the Red House Book Award and the Richard and Judy Best Children's Book for 12+, amongst others. She is also the author of *Blood Ties* and its sequel, *Blood Ransom*, *The Medusa Project* series, and the *Luke and Eve* trilogy. She has tallied up numerous award wins and has twice been longlisted for the Carnegie Medal.

@ **sophiemckenzie_**

www.facebook.com/sophiemckenzieauthor

www.sophiemckenziebooks.com